MARY JEMISON

NATIVE AMERICAN CAPTIVE

MARY JEMISON

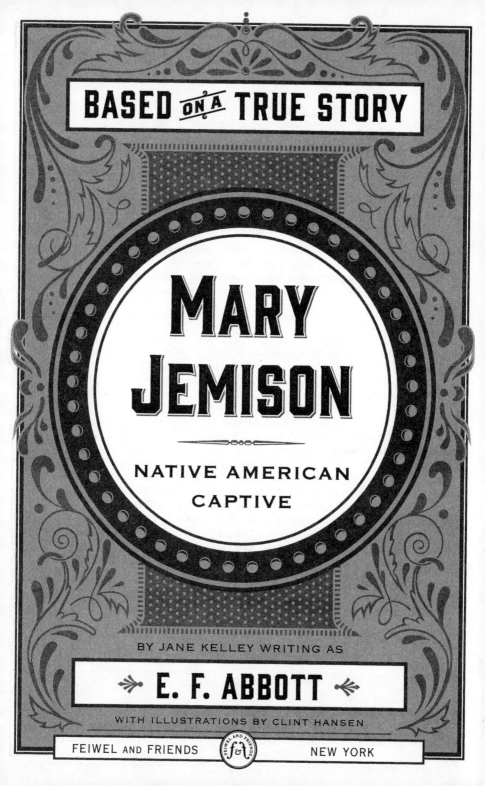

BASED ON A TRUE STORY

MARY JEMISON

NATIVE AMERICAN
CAPTIVE

BY JANE KELLEY WRITING AS

E. F. ABBOTT

WITH ILLUSTRATIONS BY CLINT HANSEN

FEIWEL AND FRIENDS   NEW YORK

A FEIWEL AND FRIENDS BOOK
An Imprint of Macmillan

MARY JEMISON: NATIVE AMERICAN CAPTIVE.
Text copyright © 2016 by Macmillan. Illustrations copyright © 2016
by Clint Hansen. All rights reserved.

Printed in the United States of America by R. R. Donnelley & Sons Company,
Harrisonburg, Virginia. For information, address Feiwel and Friends,
175 Fifth Avenue, New York, N.Y. 10010.

Our books may be purchased in bulk for promotional, educational,
or business use. Please contact your local bookseller or the Macmillan
Corporate and Premium Sales Department at (800) 221-7945 ext. 5442
or by e-mail at MacmillanSpecialMarkets@macmillan.com.

Library of Congress Cataloging-in-Publication Data
Abbott, E. F., author.
Mary Jemison : Native American captive / E. F. Abbott. — First edition.
pages cm. — (Based on a true story)
Summary: A fictional retelling of the early life of Mary Jemison who was captured
during the French and Indian War and lived for most of her life with the Seneca Indians.
ISBN 978-1-250-06838-5 (hardcover)
1. Jemison, Mary, 1743–1833—Juvenile fiction. 2. Indian captivities—Genesee River
Valley (Pa. and N.Y.)—Juvenile fiction. 3. Pioneers—Genesee River Valley (Pa. and
N.Y.)—Juvenile fiction. 4. Seneca Indians—History—Juvenile fiction. 5. Genesee
River Valley (Pa. and N.Y.)—History—Juvenile fiction. 6. United States—History—
French and Indian War, 1754–1763—Juvenile fiction. [1. Jemison, Mary, 1743–1833—
Fiction. 2. Indian captivities—Fiction. 3. Frontier and pioneer life—Genesee River
Valley (Pa. and N.Y.)—Fiction. 4. Seneca Indians—Fiction. 5. Indians of North
America—Genesee River Valley (Pa. and N.Y.)—Fiction. 6. Genesee River Valley
(Pa. and N.Y.)—History—Fiction. 7. United States—History—French and Indian
War, 1754–1763—Fiction.] I. Title.
PZ7.1.A16Mar 2016   813.6—dc23   [Fic]   201500415

Frontispiece: Photographer Ryan Hargett, licensed under a creative Commons
Attribution-ShareAlike 3.0 Unported License

Book design by Anna Booth & April Ward
Feiwel and Friends logo designed by Filomena Tuosto

First Edition: 2016

1 3 5 7 9 10 8 6 4 2

mackids.com

To Mary Jemison and her Seneca sisters. History didn't record the sisters' real names, but we do know how their courage and kindness enabled them to make a home for Mary in their hearts.

BASED ON A TRUE STORY BOOKS

are exciting historical fiction about real children who lived
through extraordinary times in American history.

———⊃∘◦∘⊂———

DON'T MISS:

John Lincoln Clem: Civil War Drummer Boy

Nettie and Nellie Crook: Orphan Train Sisters

Sybil Ludington: Revolutionary War Rider

MARY JEMISON

NATIVE AMERICAN CAPTIVE

CHAPTER 1

JULY 1743

A storm was coming. Black mountains of clouds blocked the setting sun. The ship sailed toward them. What else could it do? There was no shelter in the middle of the Atlantic Ocean.

Sailors ran around the deck, tying down whatever could be washed overboard. Waves crashed against the side of the ship. The sails flapped as the wind shifted course. Sailors chased the passengers below.

Inside the ship, the quarters were dark. There were no lights, not even a candle. Any flame could start a fire that would destroy the wooden ship. The people were crammed together on rows of cots. Many were

sick. There were fights over the sea biscuits, or if someone stumbled against another man's cot. Or about what they believed.

Many had left Ireland for America because people wouldn't be punished for their religion in William Penn's colony. But they weren't there yet.

The sea churned. The wind blew. The ship leaned to the left. Some passengers groaned. Others whispered in the dark.

"Thirty days. And still no land in sight."

"Why did we want to go to America?"

"What will we find there?"

"Land to call our own."

"Wild savages."

"Freedom."

A woman screamed.

Everyone was silent. Then there was another sound.

A tiny baby took her first breath and cried out. In the middle of the Atlantic Ocean, somewhere between the Old World and the New, Mary Jemison was born.

A beech tree stood at the edge of the farm. Mary Jemison traced the scars on its smooth gray bark with her finger.

Fifteen years ago, her father had carved his name on several trees to claim this land in central Pennsylvania. The family had worked hard to make their farm. They cut down trees and pulled stumps. They built a house and a barn. They had fields for crops, meadows where lambs and calves could wander, and an orchard dotted with pink apple blossoms.

But beyond the beech tree was a dark tangle of wilderness.

Mary patted the tree. Then she entered the shadows of the woods.

It's only a mile, Mary reminded herself. She had to go to the neighbors' farm to borrow a horse. No one else could go. Her older brothers, Tom and John, were busy plowing the field with the team of oxen. Her older sister, Betsey, was planting potatoes in the vegetable garden. Little brothers Matthew and Robert were too young. But Mary was fifteen. She could walk a mile, spend the night at the Greens', and ride back the next morning.

At least, that was what her father had said.

Only a mile, Mary thought. She stumbled over a tree root.

There were no roads between the farms, but the path was well traveled. When Mary was a little girl, she had spent a lot of time playing in the woods. She'd picked flowers and hunted for fairies like the ones in her mother's stories about Ireland.

But that changed as Mary grew older. Travelers from western Pennsylvania told frightening stories. More and more colonists were attacked by savages. Some were kidnapped or killed. Houses and barns were burned. Mary's father had said, "They want to scare us off our land. But we won't let them."

A typical farm in Pennsylvania circa 1747.
[LC-USZ62-31149]

Mary's father wasn't frightened. He said the troops would protect them. Mary wasn't so sure.

France's war with the British was also being fought in America. The savages were mostly helping the French. Four years ago, Mary's uncle John had joined the colonist soldiers. Colonel George Washington led them into battle in western Pennsylvania. But they had been defeated at Fort Necessity. Mary's uncle John was killed.

Now their neighbor Sergeant Wheelock was off with the colonist soldiers. His brother, John Wheelock, had seen the smoke from barns burning in the west. He thought the family would be safer if they stayed at Mary's house. That was why Mary had to borrow the Greens' horse—to help them move. The little Wheelock children couldn't walk very far.

Mary tightened her shawl around her shoulders. *It's only a mile*, she thought. Actually, it was less. She had been walking very fast for what seemed like forever.

Something squawked. Mary froze like a rabbit. Her heart fluttered in her chest like a bird with a broken wing. Only her eyes moved as she tried to see what or who had made the sound.

A savage would be silent. A savage would creep

quietly through the woods—until, at the very last moment, he would whoop the death yell.

Another burst of chatter came from on top of a log. Mary laughed and held out her hand to the small, striped chipmunk. "Don't be afraid."

She wished she had a bit of food to give it. She had been trying for months to tame a chipmunk as a pet. Her brothers Tom and John teased her. But Mary knew she would feel braver with a little furry friend in her apron pocket.

The chipmunk darted under the log and disappeared.

The sun was sinking behind the trees. It would be twilight soon. Maybe she better turn back. She could get the horse tomorrow. The Wheelocks could stay in their own house for a few more days, couldn't they?

The wind moaned and rattled the branches of the old oak.

Mary gathered up her skirt around her knees and ran along the path.

She must have passed the halfway point. Yes, there was the large boulder. She jumped from stone to stone to cross the creek. And there was the cave where Tom and John had found the arrowheads.

Indians had lived there before the Jemisons. Mary's father said that the Indians didn't care about the land. They didn't work hard to farm like he did. But Mary wondered, if they didn't, then why were they doing such awful things to try to get it back?

She was almost there. She could smell the smoke from the Greens' fireplace.

At least, she thought she did. What if it was another fire? What if the Greens' house was burning? What if she wasn't running to safety, but straight into danger?

Mary stopped. Her bonnet slipped down over her right eye. She couldn't see where to go or what to do. She pushed back the cloth. But something else came toward her. Something as large and white as a sheet surrounded her. Her blood turned cold. She sank down so fast, she felt as if she had dropped out of her body—and out of her world.

CHAPTER 3

Mary opened her eyes. The sun was shining. She was lying on a bed in the Greens' house. Mrs. Green helped her sit up. "We thought we lost you, Mary."

Mary shivered. She felt like she had been lost. But somehow she had found her way back. "What happened?"

"Samuel heard someone cry out in the woods. He got his gun and went to check. Scared him out of his boots to see you lying on the path, as if you were dead. But you had fainted."

Mary nodded. That happened sometimes, when everything was too much.

"Were you frightened? Did you see savages?" Mrs. Green said.

Mary shook her head. Sometimes it was more frightening not to see anything.

"Can you eat something? Maybe drink a little clabber?" Mrs. Green said.

"No, thank you." Thick, sour milk didn't appeal to Mary. She wished she could have strawberries. But the little plants didn't even have their white flowers yet.

"I better get home. Mama will be worrying. And the Wheelocks need your horse."

"They'll feel safer in your house, with your father and Tom and John there, too. Do you want to rest here a little longer?" Mrs. Green said.

"I'll be all right. It's only a mile." Mary stood up. She straightened her apron and tucked her blond curls back up under her bonnet. Mrs. Green wrapped Mary's shawl around her shoulders. Mary slowly walked outside.

Mr. Green helped Mary up onto the horse. She twisted her fingers in its mane and held on tightly. The horse left the barnyard and trotted along the dirt path. Mary kept her head low to the horse's neck so she wouldn't be hit by tree branches. As she passed the place where she had collapsed, the birds chirped and chattered. They had plenty to say. Were they talking about what had happened to Mary? She whistled to them, even though she knew birds couldn't explain anything. That was just a foolish notion.

She kicked her heels to urge the horse to go faster. She could see where the path opened up into her father's fields. She passed the beech tree.

Tom and John were carrying buckets of water toward the barn. They put them down and came to greet her. "Mary Contrary has come back!" Tom shouted.

Mary tried to scowl at him—but she couldn't hide her smile. She was very glad to see her older brothers.

John grabbed the bridle. "Mama is cooking breakfast."

"She needs your help. Even a little boy like Davy Wheelock can eat a lot." Tom helped Mary slide down from the horse's back.

"The Wheelocks are here already?"

"Mrs. Wheelock didn't want to wait for the horse," Tom said.

The news unsettled Mary. She wished they would all move east to Philadelphia. Let the wild animals and wild people have these woods.

Mr. Wheelock came out of the house. He took the horse's bridle from John. "I'll ride back to our place to get that sack of grain."

Father handed him a rifle. "Better take this gun."

"Why?" Mary said.

"Might see some wild animals I need to shoot." Mr. Wheelock got on the horse and cantered across the field toward the west. Mary watched the little clouds of dust fall back to the ground after the horse had gone.

"Help your mother, Mary. Tom and John, the animals need their breakfast, too. I've got to finish this ax handle." Father picked up a piece of wood. He swung it through the air as if he was attacking something.

"Father, we should be marching with Colonel Washington," Tom declared.

"We want revenge for Uncle John's death," said John.

"We can fight best by staying on our farm," Father replied firmly.

Mary went inside the house. She heard rhythmic pounding as her father's hammer struck the chisel to carve the wood.

The children were playing on the floor. Mrs. Wheelock was putting wood on the fire. Mrs. Jemison was standing by the hearth, stirring a large black kettle that hung over the fire. "Here you are, Mary. My goodness, you're pale. Are you all right?"

"When I was in the woods, a sheet flew toward me and wrapped me up," Mary whispered to her mother, but Betsey heard.

"You are a silly goose. What will you dream up next?" Betsey laughed.

"Does the sheet mean something, Mama?" Mary asked.

"It means you shouldn't have left me to bring in all the laundry," Betsey said.

"Do you think it was a banshee?" Mary said.

"A what?" Mrs. Wheelock said.

"An old woman in a folk story," Mama said. "We should have left those tales in Ireland. Help set the table." Mama gently moved Mary out of the way of the cooking.

As Mary put the plates and mugs on the table, she glanced out the window. She knew a banshee came to warn someone that something awful was going to happen.

On the floor next to the wood box, Robert was lining up rows of little sticks. "These are Colonel Washington's soldiers."

"These are the British troops that are here to help Colonel Washington." Matthew made another line of sticks.

"I won't play if I have to be the savages," Davy Wheelock whined.

"Then you can be the French," Robert said.

In the far corner, away from the door, Davy's little sisters were playing with Mary's old corn-husk doll, Priscilla. Betsey must have given Priscilla to them. Mary knew she should have found a better hiding place than under their bed. Mary took Priscilla away from the little girls and fussed with the

A corn-husk doll originating from the Seneca tribe. *[Catalog No: 50.1/1520, courtesy of the Division of Anthropology, American Museum of Natural History]*

lace apron. That scrap was all that was left of the shawl her mother had brought from Ireland.

The older Wheelock girl pointed to where Mary had attached the lace to the ribbon. "Those stitches aren't very straight. Mother makes us practice our stitches on a sampler."

"I'm all the way through the alphabet," the younger girl said.

"Mary's too cross for cross-stitching," Betsey said.

Betsey had two samplers hanging on the wall. In one, she had stitched a picture of their house. In another, she had made the Bible verse "Suffer the Little Children." Betsey always did everything perfectly. Mary shoved the little lace apron in the pocket of her skirt.

"Can I have the doll? She needs clothes. She isn't a savage," the older girl said.

"Betsey had no right to give you Priscilla," Mary said.

"Aren't you too old to play with dolls?" Mrs. Wheelock asked.

"I don't play with her. I just like to have her." Mary smoothed the corn-silk hair.

"Now, Mary, why can't the little ones play with your doll?" Mama asked.

There was no reason—except for Mary's hurt feelings. "Take it, then." Mary dropped the doll and walked toward the door. She would go to the barn and help Tom and John with the little lambs. The lambs were so adorable and fuzzy; they would make Mary feel better.

Suddenly, *bang!* A loud gunshot exploded close to the house. The little ones ran to their mothers. Then more shots—*Bang! Bang! Bang!*

Something thudded against the ground right outside the door.

Then there was silence.

CHAPTER 4

The wind whined like a beast trapped in the chimney.

The little ones hid in their mothers' skirts. Mary looked at her mother's face. Her usual smile of reassurance didn't come. Instead, Mama clutched her apron and whispered, "Thomas must have shot a fox that was trying to get the lambs."

But Mary knew the lambs were in the barn. The bangs had been right outside the door.

"Should we look?" Mrs. Wheelock whispered.

No, Mary thought. *Don't open the door.* What was inside was known. The cheerful plates, the kettle on the hearth, the spoons on the wooden table. These things were the same as always. But what was outside?

Mama detached Matthew and Robert from her skirt. They stood where she left them. She walked slowly toward the door. Her hand trembled as it reached for the latch. She pulled the heavy wood. The hinges creaked. She looked outside.

Through the gap, Mary could just barely see a man lying on the ground.

Mama slammed the door shut.

"What is it, Jane?" Mrs. Wheelock hissed.

"Mr. Wheelock has been shot," whispered Mama.

"Oh no!" Mrs. Wheelock gasped. The children started to cry.

"Hush, children. Quick. We must . . ." Mama didn't finish her sentence. She didn't know what to tell them to do.

Outside, men shouted. But it didn't sound like words. Then came the thud of blows. Someone moaned. Footsteps ran toward the house. The door was flung open. Mama fell back against the table.

Father stumbled into the room. His hands were tied behind his back. He wasn't wearing his hat. His

reddish hair had come
loose from his ponytail.
His blue eyes darted
back and forth around
the room. But he never
looked at the faces of
his frightened family
huddled together in
the corner.

A man strode into
the house. He wore a
deerskin jacket and breeches. His chest was bare. Most
of his hair had been shaved off. Two eagle feathers
stuck straight up from a stripe of hair along the top of
his head. The right half of his face was painted red; the
rest was blue. He brandished the ax handle that Father
had been making.

Five more men shouted as they came in. One had a
spiderweb painted on his face. He kicked over the
table. The dishes clattered to the floor.

Then four white men came in. They wore fringed
jackets and fur hats. Two had guns.

Mary was so relieved. The white men would cap-
ture the savages. Everything would be all right.

But the white man with a brown beard pointed his rifle at Father. *"Bouffe. Bouffe,"* the bearded man said.

Mary shrank back against the wall. These men were French. They wouldn't help the families. The French were fighting the British and the colonists.

They opened the cupboards and knocked over the barrels. Potatoes rolled across the floor. Grain scattered.

"Bouffe. Bouffe," the bearded man said again, and grabbed Father by the shirt and shook him.

The wild search continued. What were they looking for? What could savages want? Betsey squeezed Mary's hand so hard that Mary lost feeling in her fingers. Whatever it was, Mary hoped they would find it and leave.

Red Blue opened a barrel and found a hunk of dried meat. He shouted and held it above his head. Two savages rushed over. They filled their deerskin pouches with more meat and bread.

Of course they needed food, Mary realized. It had been a long winter. They were desperate with hunger— like bears waking up from their hibernation starving and cross. Maybe after these men took what they wanted, they would leave.

"On les prend?" The bearded man pointed to the families.

Red Blue grunted.

"On les tue?" the man with the rifle said.

Spiderweb shouted. He pretended to stab himself in the chest. Then he held out his hands and crossed them at the wrists.

The bearded man nodded.

Red Blue picked up a whip. He raised it above his head. The long black leather curled backward and then arced forward like a great snake. The sound split the air like another gunshot.

Father jumped.

The savages laughed. The bearded man grabbed Mama by the arm and flung her out of the house. Matthew and Robert shrieked and ran after her.

The man with the rifle shouted and used the end of the rifle to shove Betsey, then the Wheelocks, then Mary outside.

Mary practically tripped over the body of Mr. Wheelock. The horse lay beside him. It had been shot, too. She pulled up her skirt and moved as far away from the blood as she could.

Mary looked toward the barn. Were Tom and John

still there? The door was open. Mary tried to see inside the barn. Was that Tom's red shirt? Was that John's blond hair? Would they come to the rescue? Did they have any weapons besides pitchforks? Father's gun lay on the ground beside Mr. Wheelock. Tom was strong and John was clever, but how could they fight six savages and four Frenchmen with guns?

Red Blue saw Mary staring. He turned toward the barn. Mary quickly looked down at the buckles on her shoes. She hoped that John and Tom stayed hidden until they could run to get help.

The whip cracked.

"Allez! Allez!" the Frenchmen shouted.

A wood engraving of Native Americans attacking the British during the French and Indian War. *[LC-USZ62-120704]*

Spiderweb walked across the dirt field. Red Blue shoved Mary. She stumbled as she followed Spiderweb. She looked back over her shoulder. Betsey was behind Mary. Father was surrounded by Frenchmen. Matthew and Robert clung to Mama's skirt. Mrs. Wheelock and her children followed. Red Blue walked at the end of the line, cracking the whip.

They left the door unlatched, the dishes scattered on the floor, the fire blazing on the hearth, the porridge burning in the pot. They trampled the little flax seeds that Tom and John had just planted in the open field.

At the edge of this field was another beech tree where Father had carved his name and the date.

Thomas Jemison 1743

Spiderweb paid no attention to those marks. Nor did any of the other men.

The whip cracked.

The sheep stood in the meadow, watching the families disappear into the shadows of the woods.

CHAPTER 5

Several trails had been cut through this part of the forest. One went to the Wheelock farm. One went to the little village with the general store. One went to the church. But Spiderweb wasn't going anyplace Mary had ever been before. He led them through the underbrush. His deerskin leggings were barely scratched. Briars snagged Mary's skirt. Branches slapped her face and arms. She stumbled over the uneven ground.

At any moment, Mary expected to hear the thunder of galloping horses. Tom and John would ride up with the British army from the east. Sergeant Wheelock and the colonists would march down from the north.

Guns would fire into the air. Drums would urge the soldiers into battle. Tom and John would shout, "Let our family go!"

But none of that happened.

They trudged on and on and on.

If only Mama had listened to Mary when she told her about the banshee.

If only Father hadn't insisted they stay on the farm.

If only that farm wasn't in the wilderness.

If only Mary could have a drink of water.

If only Spiderweb would walk more slowly. Instead, he ran down a slope.

Mary couldn't keep up. She tripped on the hem of her skirt and fell to her hands and knees. Betsey helped her stand up and brushed her off. Mary was grateful for the touch of her sister's hand, but how could dirt possibly matter now?

The whip cracked.

They trudged on.

It was Father's whip. He

used it on the oxen to make them pull harder when the plow got stuck. They never actually felt the lash. They feared the cracking sound as the leather snake split the air. Father said the oxen were dumb beasts. Mary never gave them names, the way she did for every single lamb. But she felt so sorry for the oxen now. She felt so sorry for everything—including herself.

"Mama, when's breakfast?" Matthew said.

"Hssst." Red Blue warned him to be quiet.

"Soon," Mama said.

It wasn't.

They trudged on. And on. And on. They didn't stop to eat. They passed by a muddy pond without getting a drink of water.

Spiderweb had a large pouch slung from his shoulder. Mary stared at the bulges of the deerskin pouch. She knew the savages had stolen meat and bread from their kitchen. Why didn't they let the families eat? Couldn't they see how hungry and tired the children were? Didn't they care how anyone suffered? Why had they taken the families? Why did they want little whimpering children?

The whip cracked.

They struggled up a rocky cliff. At the bottom, far away, water gushed along a stream. Mary's mouth was as dry and dusty as the trail. Her tongue stuck to the roof of her mouth.

The sun was now above their heads.

"The children could walk better if they had water and rest," Mama said.

"Hssst," Red Blue said.

The top of the cliff would be above the trees. When they reached it, Mary would be able to see Tom and John. Even if they were miles away, the bright red jackets of the British soldiers would jump to her eyes from the muted colors of the woods.

Mary climbed faster and faster. She stumbled over a loose rock and fell to her knees again. She pushed herself back up. She stood at the top of the cliff. She looked past Betsey, past Father's stricken face, past Mama's red hair straggling from her bonnet, and past the whip slashing through the air. Mary could see the entire valley. An endless sea of brown and green.

There were no red uniforms marching to the rescue. Mary blinked back her tears. She couldn't even see a field or a farmhouse from which help could come.

The whip cracked.

As they walked downhill, the littlest Wheelock girl stumbled and slid all the way down. She sat and cried with her arms up. Mary trudged past. She barely had the strength to lift her own feet. Mrs. Wheelock grabbed the little girl and carried her.

They were back in the forest. The trees and bushes closed around them. Thorns caught at Mary's skirt. She didn't try to untangle the fabric. She was too tired. She heard it tear as she plodded on.

The shadows grew longer. The sun would soon set. The longest day of her life was ending. The savages would have to stop soon. Not even they could walk all night. Could they? There had been no breakfast, no lunch, no water, no dinner. Maybe there would be no rest.

Up ahead, an orange light pierced the shadows of the trees. Was it a cabin? A campfire? Mary walked a little faster toward that glow. Then she stopped. It wasn't anyone who could help. It was the sun's last burst of color.

When the sun sank below the trees, it took hope with it.

"We keep going west," Betsey said.

Mary nodded. Their captors were taking them farther away from villages and churches and settled land. They might already have passed the abandoned Fort Necessity. The only people they might meet would be French and Indians. No one who would help.

Gloom spread quickly from the shadows of the trees. The birds sang in the twilight, but eventually they fell silent.

The whip cracked.

The families stumbled among the shadows. Mary remembered the forest was full of other beasts to fear.

Finally, Spiderweb held up his hand.

"Arrêtez," the man with the rifle said.

They stopped.

Mary sank to her knees. She crawled over to where Mama held Matthew and Robert. The Jemisons pressed against one another for what comfort they could find.

The Frenchmen and the warriors sat a few yards away. They stared at the families.

Mary waited for them to light a fire. They didn't move. Mary couldn't see their faces in the dark, but she felt their eyes.

"Breakfast, Mama?" Matthew whispered.

This time, Mama didn't say "Soon." She shook her head.

No breakfast, no lunch, no dinner, no water. But now they could rest their weary legs and somehow, hopefully, escape into sleep.

Mary lay on the hard ground and looked up through the branches at the sky. The little points of light were so far away. Could they be the same stars she used to see from the farm before everything had changed?

CHAPTER 6

A wolf howled. The animal's cry sounded much louder out here in the forest. Mary sat up and looked around. She couldn't distinguish one dark shape from another.

"How? How?" the wolf cried.

Mary asked herself the same thing. How? How could they keep going? How long would they have to suffer? How would they ever get home?

One of the Wheelock girls whimpered. Matthew sniffed. He was trying to be brave. They all were. But how long could they keep from crying?

Mama hummed under her breath. Mary recognized the tune. Father and Mama used to dance to this

Irish jig. Tom and John would compete to see who could kick the highest. Betsey would swing Matthew around. Robert would step on Mary's toes.

But a warrior hissed. Mama sighed and was silent for the rest of the night.

The skies were gray. The sun hadn't even risen. Red Blue prodded them with the end of the whip. The families struggled to stand on their stiff legs.

The Frenchmen argued with the warriors. The man with the rifle pointed angrily at the little children. Their quarrel made Mary anxious. What did they want to do? She almost felt relieved when Spiderweb motioned with his arm.

The whip cracked. The march began again. Mary's skirt was torn. Her feet were sore. She felt dizzy from lack of food. But she could endure these sufferings. As long as they were walking, nothing terrible could happen to them. At least, that was what she hoped.

The sun peeked up above the trees. The gray shadows changed to pale greens. The birds sang. Mama didn't.

They came to a stream. Red Blue knelt to drink from his hands. So did the other warriors and the Frenchmen. Finally, Spiderweb motioned. The families rushed to the edge. Davy Wheelock was so eager that he tumbled in. The warriors laughed. Mary dipped her hands into the stream. The cool liquid glided down the back of her throat. She had never appreciated how wonderful water was.

Spiderweb opened up the pouch. He took out the bread and the meat stolen from the Jemisons' kitchen. The children greedily crammed the food in their mouths. Mary and Betsey ate more slowly. Father's head hung down. He refused his share.

"Eat, Thomas, please. We need your strength," Mama whispered in his ear.

The bread caught against a lump in Mary's throat. They did need his strength. But he had none to give.

"We don't know what lies ahead," Mama whispered.

Father grunted as if he knew but didn't want to say.

Spiderweb jumped to his feet. Red Blue cracked the whip. The families marched on, in the same order as before.

Mary tried to keep a little water in her mouth. But soon even the memory of it was gone. Her tongue was once again as dusty as the ground.

When the sun was high in the sky, they passed a tall fence made of logs. Mary's heart pounded with excitement. Maybe Spiderweb had gotten confused by the woods. Maybe he had mistakenly led them to people who would help.

"Fort Canagojigge," Father muttered.

Now Mary could see the fort was deserted. Soldiers had abandoned it. And once again Mary gave up her hope of rescue.

They trudged on. Up a ridge and down the other side. Mile after mile, with no end in sight.

The man with the rifle whispered angrily at the warriors. Mary tried to understand what he was saying. *Yengeese* almost sounded like a French word for "English." The rest of the words were just angry grunts. The voices got louder and louder.

"Hssst." Spiderweb held up his hand. The warriors were instantly silent. They stared back the way they had come. Mary looked, too, but the forest hid all from her eyes.

Red Blue pushed through a tangle of thick bushes. Thorns again tore Mary's skirt. Her bonnet caught on a branch. She was too tired to retrieve it. Betsey put it back on Mary's head. They passed through a dark and dismal swamp, where their feet sank into the muck as they walked among the gloomy hemlock trees.

After entering a forest, Spiderweb pointed at the ground, so the families sat.

Three Feathers opened his pouch of food. No one wanted to eat—not even the children. Mama broke off small bites of bread and placed them in Robert's mouth, as if he was a baby bird.

Mary wished they were all birds. Then they could fly away. No one forced birds to trudge through the woods without any hint of where they were going. Or what might happen to them when they arrived.

"Come now, eat," Mama said. "We worked hard to make this bread."

A tear came to Mary's eye. They had worked hard. Father had grown the wheat. Tom and John had harvested the grain. Betsey and Mary had ground the flour. Mama had mixed the dough. Even Matthew and Robert had punched the loaves to help them rise.

They managed to swallow a few bites—except Father, who just shook his head.

Three Feathers put the leftovers back in his pouch. Spiderweb stood up. The children groaned. They couldn't take one more step that night.

Spiderweb circled around the families, staring at each person with dark, expressionless eyes. He moved silently, as if he was stalking his prey. Then he stopped directly in front of Mary.

Mary shrank back against her mother.

Spiderweb grabbed her ankle. She tried to pull away her foot, but his grip was strong. Mary clung to Betsey's hand. But Spiderweb didn't try to drag Mary off. He fumbled with the buckle on her shoe.

"Mama?" Mary cried softly.

"He wants your shoe," Mama whispered.

Mary nearly laughed. Her shoes were so old. Betsey had worn them for years. When her toes pinched, the shoes were given to Mary. They had never been shiny. After trudging through the woods and the swamp, the leather was caked with mud.

"Why?" Mary whispered.

Mama stroked Mary's hair and started humming again. This time the song she chose was a hymn.

Spiderweb yanked off Mary's left shoe.

Mary curled her toes. There was a hole in her stocking. But no one saw. Spiderweb ripped off the stocking. Then he removed her right shoe.

Mary's feet looked white and pale against the muddy ground. The air felt cold. She shivered. How would she walk barefoot?

Then Spiderweb reached in his pouch and took out a pair of shoes made from deerskin, like the ones the warriors wore. He put them on Mary's feet. The deerskin felt soft. The sides were fringed. On the top, someone had sewn several rows of white beads.

"Moccasins." Mama turned to her husband. She shook his arm. "Thomas. He gave Mary moccasins. You know what that means."

Father buried his face in his hands.

"What do they mean, Mama?" Mary whispered.

Mama tried to keep humming, but her voice broke.

A pair of moccasins made by the Iroquois in the early eighteenth century. [*Wikimedia Commons, author Daderot*]

Three Feathers took the shoes off Davy Wheelock's feet.

"Are we all getting moccasins?" Mary whispered.

Betsey tucked her feet under her skirt. "I want to keep my shoes."

Spiderweb stood in front of Mary. He motioned with his arm.

Mama squeezed Mary's hand until it hurt. "Mary, you must prepare yourself. If they are giving you moccasins, I think they will let you live. Although how you *will* live, I can't imagine," Mama whispered.

"What about you?" Mary asked.

"We will go to heaven," Mama answered softly.

"No!" Mary cried.

Spiderweb tried to make Mary get up. Mary clutched her mother's arms.

Spiderweb raised his arm above Mary's head. He had a stone ax in his hand.

Mama detached Mary's hands from her arm. "Mary, you must go with him."

"Go?" Mary shrieked. "How can I go?"

"Be brave, my poor little girl. Say your prayers every day. No matter what they try to make you do," Mama said.

"What will they make me do?" Mary asked.

Three Feathers grabbed Davy from his mother. Mrs. Wheelock and her little girls were sobbing, too.

Spiderweb took Mary's arm. His fingers dug all the way to her bone.

"Listen to me, Mary," commanded Mama. "Don't even try to escape. Or they will kill you, too. And you must live, Mary. Live so someone will remember our names."

Mary's shoulders shook. She shut her eyes, but nothing could stop her tears.

Spiderweb dragged Mary and Davy Wheelock away from their families and deeper into the forest.

CHAPTER 7

*T*homas, Jane, Tom, John, Betsey, Matthew, Robert.

Thomas, Jane, Tom, John, Betsey, Matthew, Robert.

Mary whispered her family's names as she followed Spiderweb. At first she was crying so much, she could hardly walk over the rough ground. Her feet slid inside the moccasins. She could feel every stick and stone through the soft leather of the soles.

Davy was crying, too.

Thomas, Jane, Tom, John, Betsey, Matthew, Robert.

"Hssst." Spiderweb raised his arm to threaten Mary.

Mary bit her lip and was silent. Then she could hear her mother singing a hymn. Mama was trying to send her comfort. That reminded Mary she couldn't go on without her. How could she walk? Each step took her farther from her family. But Mama had told her to be brave. Somehow, Mary put one foot in front of the other. The melody got fainter and fainter until it was just a memory.

Thomas, Jane, Tom, John, Betsey, Matthew, Robert.

They climbed up a small hill and down the other side. They crossed a stream. Spiderweb stopped by a fallen tree. He pointed to the children and to the ground.

Mary lay down on the dirt and covered her face with her hands. Davy lay down next to her. She felt his anxious breathing. She reached over to pat his trembling arm. A sob escaped from him.

"Hssst." Spiderweb sat cross-legged a few yards away from them.

Mary turned to avoid looking at him. But she could feel his eyes.

Thomas, Jane, Tom, John, Betsey, Matthew, Robert.

Davy whispered in her ear. "We should go back. We can run while he's sleeping."

"He isn't sleeping," Mary replied.

"I can't stay here. I'm too scared," Davy whimpered.

"We have to. We don't know where we are or which way to run. We'd be lost," whispered Mary.

"We *are* lost," Davy said.

Mary rolled onto her back and looked up through the tree branches. The stars made a glittering path. She wished she could follow it to heaven. Especially if that was where her mother would be.

"I'm going to run. I have to." Davy sat up.

From somewhere in the darkness came a terrible scream.

Davy grabbed Mary's arm. "Mama?"

"It's a panther," Mary whispered. But it wasn't much more comforting to think of the large beast prowling among the trees.

Davy lay back down.

Mary pulled some dried leaves over them. She shut her eyes and prayed, *Please let me sleep.* Eventually, she forgot the hard ground and whatever might be happening in the dark forest, and slept.

———◈◈◈———

The sky was promisingly pink when Mary heard footsteps hurrying toward them. She shook Davy awake. "Our families are coming."

They stood together, holding hands. Through the trees, Mary saw people coming. Her mother was mistaken. The moccasins didn't mean anything. They all would live.

"Look, it's Father." Mary could see Mr. Jemison's blue jacket. He led the group, as he always used to do. He came around some bushes and into the clearing. Then Mary screamed.

He had a warrior's face.

Red Blue was wearing Mr. Jemison's jacket.

"What have you done with my father?" Mary shouted. But she knew. She could see. Dark blood stained the blue fabric, right where the heart should be.

Three Feathers came next. Then the other warriors and the four Frenchmen. And no one else.

Spiderweb said something to Red Blue. Red Blue reached into his pouch. He held up several chunks of hair. Red, blond, brown.

Mary gasped and held on to Davy. She recognized those colors. Now there could be no doubt. Her family would not be trudging through the woods with her. They were in heaven.

Red Blue cracked the whip. Spiderweb pulled Mary away from Davy.

The march began again.

Three Feathers crept behind the group, using a long pole to lift up the grass their feet had trampled. The warriors were making sure no one could follow their trail.

Was someone searching for them? Could they rescue them? Did it even matter now? Her family was gone. It was too late to save them. It was too late.

Thomas, Jane, Tom, John, Betsey, Matthew, Robert. And Mary.

She added her own name to the list. She was lost as well.

An hour passed. And then a day. Snow began to fall. Mary was so cold, she couldn't feel her feet. She stuck her hands in her pockets under her apron, where she found the little scrap of lace attached to the ribbon with her crooked stitches. She fingered the lace her mother had made. But Mary couldn't cry anymore. She was numb.

The forest stretched on and on and on. How many miles had they trudged? Were they still in Pennsylvania? Were they still on the earth?

Thomas, Jane, Tom, John, Betsey, Mary, Matthew, Robert.

Another day, another night. Three Feathers killed a deer. Spiderweb handed her a chunk of roasted meat. She ate. After the warmth of the fire thawed her arms and legs, her tears flowed again.

Spiderweb stared at her.

Mary stared back. She no longer cared if he saw her cry.

Spiderweb put on a little act. He started walking slowly and low to the ground, as if pretending to be a child. Then he looked back, as if he was being chased. He wanted Mary to understand something. She refused to even try. Her family had been killed. And now Mary was all alone.

Thomas, Jane, Tom, John, Betsey, Mary, Matthew, Robert.

The next day, Mary didn't get up.

The fire had gone out. The ashes were cold and gray. Mary felt like those ashes, like something that no longer was.

Spiderweb raised his arm threateningly above Mary's head.

Mary shut her eyes. She couldn't go on. She wouldn't. There was no point.

Then she heard a blue jay squawk. She looked up at

the bird perched on the branch of a tree. It squawked again. She was certain it said, *"Live."*

How? Mary wondered.

It didn't tell her how. It squawked again, *"Live."*

So she struggled to her feet and followed Spider-web.

The blue jay flew along with them. It pecked at the buds on the trees. It continued to squawk at Mary. Its raucous cry was nothing like her mother's kind voice. And yet Mary believed her mother was somehow finding a way to remind Mary: *"Live."*

She fingered the scrap of lace in her pocket. "I will, Mama. I will."

Thomas, Jane, Tom, John, Betsey, Mary, Matthew, Robert.

When the sun was low in the west, Mary heard a loud sound of water rushing. They must be close to a large river. Three Feathers no longer bothered to hide their trail.

"Monongahela." Spiderweb pointed to a shining ribbon of water. The setting sun seemed to set the river

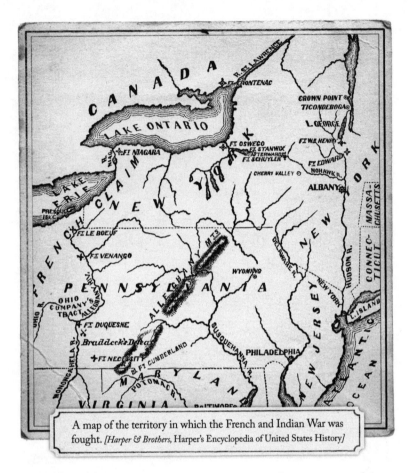

A map of the territory in which the French and Indian War was fought. [*Harper & Brothers*, Harper's Encyclopedia of United States History]

on fire. The river was nearly as wide as one of her father's fields. Her heart pounded with excitement. Rivers were like roads in the country. A river as large as this one must have people. Maybe they could help Mary and Davy.

Up ahead, the river forked around a point of land.

Near the river's edge was a large fort in the shape of a star. A flag flew from the top of a tower. From this distance, the colors were hard to see. Was it a British flag? Had there been a battle? Had the British captured the fort?

"Duquesne!" the Frenchmen shouted as they ran ahead.

The flag was blue, but it didn't have the British red cross. It had three strange golden flowers.

Spiderweb took a small clay pot out of his pouch. He dipped his fingers inside. When he pulled them out, they were bloodred. He stretched his red hand toward Mary. She shut her eyes. She felt him knock off her bonnet. He grabbed her head. His fingertips slowly stroked her hair. They slid down her right cheek, then the left. He did this three more times. Then he released her.

She watched him paint Davy's face and hair red.

What did the marks mean? What would happen to them now?

The warriors whooped. They shook their weapons at the sky. They danced and chanted as they brought their prisoners inside the fort.

CHAPTER 8

Mary and Davy sat on the floor. Just beyond the wall, warriors whooped and women chanted. The sound of rattles jangled Mary's nerves. The pounding drums throbbed inside her bones.

"Mary? Are you sorry we were spared?" Davy said.

Mary didn't answer. What good did it do to be sorry? Besides, they might not really be.

The door opened. They both stood up, expecting the worst.

A man stumbled into the room. The door slammed shut again. The man sank to the floor. His clothes were dirty and torn. His red jacket had no buttons. He had moccasins on his feet. This man was a prisoner, too. "English?" he said.

"Yes," Mary said.

"Are you a soldier?" Davy said.

The man looked at his jacket and stuck his finger through a long rip. "I was."

"Are there other soldiers close by? Will they attack the fort?" Mary said.

"Maybe. If they can take Fort Duquesne, they can

Fort Duquesne [renamed Fort Pitt following British capture] as it appeared in 1902. *[LC-USZ62-20045]*

control the Ohio River and everything west of here," the man said.

"Then we'll be saved?" Mary asked hopefully.

"I said they'd try to. I didn't say they could. Most of the tribes are fighting on the side of the French," the man replied.

"Why don't the tribes stay in their wilderness and leave us alone?" Mary said.

"The warrior who caught me said the British and the French are like two sides of a scissors. The tribes are the cloth that's cut to pieces between them."

Mary fingered the lace in her pocket. She couldn't feel sorry for the tribes. Not after what they'd done.

They all listened to the whooping outside the room. The drums beat faster and louder—like a wild horse galloping out of control.

"What will they do with us?" wondered Mary.

"Let's hope they've had enough vengeance," the man said.

Davy whimpered.

Mary thought about what had happened to her family. She wiped the tears off her cheeks. Now the red paint stained her fingertips.

The drumming got so loud, they couldn't hear one

another speak. She tried to say the names of her family, but she could only think, *Ven-geance. Ven-geance. Vengeance.*

Hours passed. Between the cracks in the log walls, Mary could see the flicker of firelight. The drums continued all night. Finally, just before dawn, they stopped.

The door opened. Spiderweb and Red Blue led them to an open space in the center of the fort. Mary, Davy, and the man stood next to the charred ashes from last night's bonfire. The dancers and chanters were gone. A few members of the tribes had begun the day's work. Some dragged firewood to a pile by the fence. Others carried baskets of food. Others cleaned their guns. Everyone stared at the prisoners.

Two Frenchmen approached Red Blue and Spiderweb. They pointed to the prisoners and spoke rapidly in French. *"On veut les hommes Yengeese."*

The Frenchmen gave some beads and bullets to Spiderweb. Red Blue examined the amount. He nodded.

The Frenchmen dragged Davy and the man toward the fort entrance. The tall doors opened, and the Frenchmen shoved Davy and the man outside. Then the doors banged shut.

"Davy!" Mary shouted. But she was too late. The last person who actually knew her was gone. And she hadn't really said good-bye.

Mary stroked the rough edges of the lace. She didn't know how to prepare herself for whatever her fate would be. Mama had told her to pray, so Mary tried. *Our Father, who art in heaven.* She stopped. Her father really was in heaven now. So was her mother.

Thomas, Jane, Tom, John, Betsey, Mary, Matthew, Robert.

Two native women were staring at Mary. They weren't much older than she was. Their tunics and leggings were made of deerskin. The tall one had a nose like a sharp beak. Her shiny black hair was tightly braided. Her part had been painted red. The shorter one had a rounder face. She wore a collar of white and yellow feathers. Her hair hung loose almost to her waist. The women walked around Mary. Braids peered closely at Mary and made disapproving clucks.

Would they take her? And if they did, what would they do to her? Would they make Mary a slave? Or would they do something even worse?

Braids spoke to Spiderweb and gave him some beads. He frowned and shook his head. Braids chattered angrily and pointed at Mary's torn clothes. Clearly, she didn't think Mary was worth any more. Spiderweb shrugged and nodded.

Mary belonged to them now.

The native women took Mary outside the fort. They dragged her to the edge of the river and put her in the center of a wooden canoe. Braids got in the back and pushed off from the land. They chanted "O-hi-o, O-hi-o" as they paddled.

They rounded a bend. Fort Duquesne disappeared from view. The river passed through a dense forest. Now the current was so strong, the women hardly had to paddle. Mary clung to the wooden crossbars of the canoe. She was swept along. Forces much more powerful than she was determined her fate. Where were they going? What would happen to her when they arrived?

A deer was getting a drink at the edge of the river. He raised his head. His big brown eyes looked sorrowfully at Mary as she passed.

Mama had told Mary not to try to escape. But the situation had changed. Now Mary was with two women.

Could she swim to shore? If she survived the icy water, then what would happen to her in the forest?

Mary didn't know what to do. A stronger girl would fight back. A smarter girl would escape.

Up ahead, Mary could see a high wall made of logs. They were approaching another fort. Something red waved from the top of a pole. Was it the British flag?

"Help! Help!" Mary leaned over the edge toward the fort. The canoe tipped dangerously to that side.

Braids used her paddle to push Mary back into the center of the canoe.

"He-eh Yengeese!" Braids shouted.

"Help!" Mary screamed again.

As they got closer, Mary could see the red cloth wasn't a flag at all. It was the remnants of a burned red coat. The wooden walls were charred. Several dead bodies lay on the ground. Their arms and legs were sprawled across the muddy shore, as if they were still trying to escape.

CHAPTER 9

When the sun was directly overhead, they came to a place where a smaller river joined the Ohio. Two children were playing on the bank. They were dressed in deerskin tunics. When they saw the canoe, they shouted and waved. "Odankot! Jako-ki!"

Feathers waved her paddle in the air and shouted, "Jis-ta-ah! Ha-no-wa!"

Braids reached out with her paddle and pulled it toward her to turn the canoe. Now both women dug deep into the water to paddle up the smaller river. The children ran along a path, keeping pace with the canoe. The boy looked to be about the age of Matthew. He had a few feathers in his short black hair.

The girl was older. She had a beaded choker around her neck. They both stared at Mary.

Braids scolded the children. They waded into the water and guided the canoe to a sandy spot. Feathers got out. The boy helped her pull the canoe halfway up on the shore. He held the canoe while Feathers and the girl hurried up a path.

Braids pushed Mary. Mary guessed she was supposed to get out of the canoe. She did as she was told.

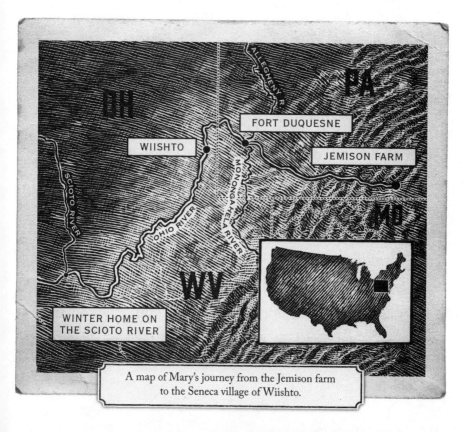

A map of Mary's journey from the Jemison farm to the Seneca village of Wiishto.

More native women and children came over to stare at Mary. Some had babies strapped to boards on their backs. Two of the women carried the canoe up the path. Mary started to follow them. Braids grabbed Mary's skirt and pulled her in the opposite direction, toward the Ohio River.

Braids snatched off Mary's shawl. Mary's skirt was in tatters from the days in the woods. As the woman ripped it off, Mary quickly put her hand in the pocket and clenched the scrap of lace in her fist. Braids tore off Mary's blouse. Mary clung to her last bit of clothing, but Braids was too strong. She ripped off Mary's petticoat. Mary was completely naked. She tried to cover herself with her hands. Her face flushed red with shame. Braids bundled up Mary's clothes and heaved them out into the river. The native women cheered and shouted.

Mary stood shivering on the shore, watching her real self float away. The clothes sank. Mary's heart sank with them.

Braids dragged Mary into the river. Mary was certain that she would be drowned. But the woman dipped her hand in the water and rubbed Mary's arms and legs. She pointed to Mary's face. After Mary scrubbed the red paint off her cheeks, Braids helped Mary out of the water.

Feathers stood on the shore with an armful of clothes. Braids handed Mary a tunic and leggings made of deerskin. Mary put them on, careful to keep the scrap of lace in her fist. The deerskin was stiffer than cloth, but it was much warmer than what Mary had been wearing.

Braids took Mary's arm and led her up the path to a fence made of vertical logs. Inside was a village. There were two rows of rectangular houses covered with bark. Smoke came out of several holes in each roof. The houses were about twice as tall as a man, and about six times as long. They had no windows, just a deerskin door at each end. In the center of the village there was one house that was bigger than the others. Next to it was a tall wooden pole.

Mary Jemison dressed in the clothing of the Seneca.
[James E. Seaver, The Life of Mary Jemison, De-He-Wa-Mis*]*

An Iroquois longhouse. While some had arched roofs, others were peaked. *[E. A. Allen, The Prehistoric World: or, Vanished Races]*

From inside the house, a drum started beating in a slow, ponderous march.

All the women and children stopped chattering. They solemnly entered this largest house. Braids nudged Mary to follow.

It was hard to see in the darkness. The fire burning in the center of the house gave off more smoke than flame. There was one big room full of about fifty people. Some sat close to the fire. Some sat on small cots in the shadows. Ears of corn and gourds and baskets hung from the rafters.

Braids pushed Mary to sit on the ground near the fire. She sat on Mary's left. Feathers sat on Mary's right.

An old woman with a beaded necklace sprinkled dried leaves on the fire. Clouds of black smoke rose up. The old woman waved the smoke up toward the hole in the ceiling. The smoke stung Mary's eyes. She rubbed them with the fist that held the scrap of lace.

Suddenly, the old woman flung her arms up over her head and wailed.

It was a horrible sound. It was the howl of a wolf. It was the sob of great loss. It was Mary being torn from her mother's arms. She felt waves of misery, but she dared not cry. No matter what happened, she would keep her face as hard as stone. She clenched her fist tighter around the lace.

Then all the women gave voice to their suffering. The wails were so loud that Mary felt the ears of dried corn tremble.

The old woman started chanting. A younger woman acted out her words. The younger woman danced around the fire. Then she crept slowly as if she was stalking a deer. She shot the deer with an imaginary bow and arrow. She lifted her arms in thanks. Then someone else stood up and pretended to shoot the hunter woman. She died a horrible death. The old woman's chanting became wailing.

The drums beat louder. Someone shook a turtle-shell rattle.

Now all the women held out their hands, as if to say, *Why? Why? Why?*

The hunter woman pointed accusingly at Mary.

Mary shook her head. She hadn't done anything wrong.

Now the rest of the women pointed at Mary.

Mary shrank back. They were blaming her because she was white. A white man must have killed the hunter. It didn't matter that Mary had never hurt anyone. Or that Mary's own family had been murdered. That wasn't enough suffering. The women wanted more. The moaning and shrieking got louder and angrier.

Braids stood up. She had a knife in one hand. She grabbed hold of Mary's hair with the other.

This was the end, Mary thought. She had been dragged through the forest only to die here in this horrible place. She lived just long enough to suffer the loss of her family. She shut her eyes. *Thomas, Jane, Tom, John, Betsey, Mary, Matthew, Robert.*

The wailing stopped. The rattle of the bones stopped. The drumming slowed to a steady thump.

Someone was singing. The music sounded like the somber coo of a mourning dove.

Braids released Mary's hair. Mary opened her eyes.

Feathers smiled as she sang. She knelt near the place on the ground where the hunter had fallen. Then she lifted her arms up with the rising smoke. She moved her arms in a great arc as if she was painting a rainbow.

The other women started singing and swaying gently like the branches of a tree. They walked in a great circle clockwise around the fire. Each time they stepped with one foot, they tapped the ground lightly with the other. Step-pat, step-pat, step-pat. They smiled at Mary as they passed. While they danced, the old woman with the beads chanted again, but now her words sounded calm.

Mary was confused. What had happened to their anger? Where had it gone? Would it come back?

"Deh-ge-wan-us," the old woman said.

"Deh-ge-wan-us," all the women said.

Feathers pointed to Mary's lips. She wanted Mary to say the word, too.

Mary opened her mouth to speak. Instead, a great sob burst from her. She shut her mouth and bit her lip.

Maybe these women had suffered the loss of a loved one. Somehow this ceremony had helped them find peace. Mary didn't think that would be possible for her. These women still had other friends and family. They weren't like Mary—utterly alone.

CHAPTER 10

HE SATA

The Moon When Plants Grow Again

The women led Mary into another slightly smaller bark house. Wooden partitions on each side of a long passage divided the house into three sections. At the center of each section was a fire. Mary was made to sit by the fire closest to the entrance.

The women taught Mary their names. Braids was called Jako-ki. Feathers was Odankot. The old woman was named Hi-hi-ih. Jako-ki chattered to the others. Her words flowed around Mary in an endless stream of syllables. Their language was so different from hers. So many *hah*s and *heh*s. The only word that sounded at all familiar was *Yengeese*. And that, she could tell, by the hiss of that *s*, meant "English." Like Mary. She thought she might have been given a new name. Deh? Duh? Dah? Unfortunately, Mary couldn't remember what it was.

Odankot smiled at her. Mary was grateful that these women seemed kind. But Mary's face felt as stiff as her old shoes. Where were her shoes now? she wondered. Had the warrior kept them? It bothered her that she didn't know. She needed to remember these things. She had to hang on to what she knew.

Thomas, Jane, Tom, John, Betsey, Mary, Matthew, Robert. Thomas, Jane, Tom, John, Betsey, Mary, Matthew, Robert. Thomas, Jane, Tom, John, Betsey . . .

———◆◆◆———

When Mary opened her eyes, she was covered by a strange blanket made of vines and feathers. She didn't know where it had come from. She remembered walking through the forest with savages. She remembered her mother had died and turned into a blue jay. No, that couldn't be true. It must be a terrible nightmare. Her mother wasn't dead. Mary could smell porridge cooking. She sat up.

A woman was bent over a kettle.

"Mama?" Mary said.

The old woman turned around and smiled. Her black eyes were almost hidden by her wrinkled brown skin. Black braids looped around her ears.

"Who are you?" Mary said.

"Hi-hi-ih." The old woman pointed to herself.

Now Mary remembered everything. Her family had been killed by the savages. Two native women had taken Mary from the fort and brought her to this dark place.

Hi-hi-ih used a wooden ladle to scoop porridge into a bark bowl. She gave the bowl and a wooden spoon to Mary. Mary took a small bite. There was something hard in the porridge. Mary looked more closely at what she was eating. The lumps were kernels of corn! Back home, only the animals ate corn. Back home, Mama made porridge from grain. But home didn't exist anymore.

Hi-hi-ih was watching. Mary tried to swallow. The corn lumps couldn't get past the bigger lumps in her throat.

Hi-hi-ih spoke. But of course Mary didn't understand. Then Hi-hi-ih smiled. She put her finger to her lips, as if to caution Mary not to say anything. Hi-hi-ih reached into a basket that hung from one of the rafters.

She took out a lump of dirt. She crumbled it into Mary's bowl. She gestured that Mary should eat.

Mary sighed. She remembered her own mother urging them to eat. To be strong enough to face whatever the day would bring. For her mother's sake, Mary took a bite.

The mush tasted like maple sugar. Mary remembered how just a few months ago, Father had drilled holes in the trunks of the maple trees. He hung buckets to catch the sap. Mama boiled the sap until it was a thick brown syrup. It cooled into lumps of sugar.

But where did Hi-hi-ih get the sugar? The natives must have done what Mary's family did. And Hi-hi-ih had also known how to coax a child to eat.

After Mary had finished her breakfast, Hi-hi-ih led Mary along a path to a field. It was only one-quarter the size of Mary's father's smallest field. There were no men. A long line of women were working in the dirt.

"Dehgewanus," Odankot shouted, and waved at Mary. In the sunlight, her collar of feathers glowed.

"Dehgewanus." Jako-ki made a snoring sound and rested her cheek on her hands as if she was asleep.

The women laughed as they poked at the ground

with long sticks. At the end of each stick was a flat piece of old animal bone. No wonder these women didn't have a large field. They didn't have oxen to pull a plow, like the Jemisons did.

These women chattered and laughed. But Mary seemed to hear the crack of the whip that had forced the families to trudge through the forest.

Hi-hi-ih led Mary to the edge of the field, where many children were playing. Then she said several words to them, including the word "Dehgewanus."

"Dehgewanus," the children said.

Why did everyone keep saying that word? Then Mary realized "Dehgewanus" must be her name now.

Hi-hi-ih pointed to the children. Mary guessed she was supposed to watch over them. She felt relieved. She could do that.

A girl curled one lock of Mary's yellow hair around her finger and yanked. Mary cried out, "Ow!"

A boy laughed. He took the girl's braid and yanked. "Ow!" the girl said.

The boy smiled and pointed to them. "Ow, Dehgewanus. Ow, Jis-ta-ah."

"Ow, Ha-no-wa." Jis-ta-ah pulled the boy's hair.

He kept his face like a stone—until Jis-ta-ah tickled him.

The women had piled old cornstalks at the edge of the field. Ha-no-wa and the other boys threw the stalks as spears. Jis-ta-ah and the girls folded the dried leaves into dolls. Jis-ta-ah tried to tie grass around her doll, but her grass was too short. Mary gave her a longer piece of grass and showed her how to tie a bow.

Jis-ta-ah danced her doll happily around Mary.

Mary took the doll. Tears came to her eyes. "I had a doll just like this. Her name was Priscilla and she didn't know how happy she was until it had all been taken away. She's probably burned now, because when they took us away, the fire was in the hearth."

"He-eh Yengeese!" Jako-ki shouted. Her black braids slapped against her back as she ran across the field to scold Mary.

"I'm sorry, I'm sorry." Mary spread her hands. What had she done? Had the boys been too wild? Had she lost one of the children? "What did I do wrong?"

Jako-ki shook her hand back and forth. "He-eh Yengeese!"

"I said I was sorry. I don't know how else to say it."

Then Mary realized that was her mistake. She had spoken English.

"He-eh Yengeese," Jako-ki said firmly.

Tears came. Mary quickly blinked them back. She had to do what they said. She had no choice. She nodded.

Jako-ki nodded and walked back across the field.

But Mary knew that if she couldn't speak her language, she would have no words.

CHAPTER 11

And so Mary did not speak.

When Hi-hi-ih gave Mary a bark bowl of corn stew, Mary nodded her head in thanks. When the children played too close to the river, Mary waved her arms to shoo them back. When Odankot smiled at Mary, Mary tried to make her mouth smile back. When Jako-ki taught Mary words by pointing at things, Mary listened. She learned *kah-kaw* meant "moon." *Dion-dot* meant "tree." *Seneca* was the name of this tribe. *Wiishto* was the name of this village.

But Mary didn't speak. What good were those words? They couldn't begin to express how she felt. Inside her head, her thoughts roared like the wind tearing at the branches of the trees. *Why am I here? Why did I live? Why should I live? Thomas Jane Tom John Betsey Mary Matthew Robert. Mama Mama Mama.*

Days passed. Many things were the same. The women worked in the field. Mary watched the children. Everyone gathered wood for the fire to cook the dinner of corn and meat. But each day, the sun climbed higher in the sky. And each night, the moon came later. Each night, the moon was smaller. Then one night, it didn't come at all.

The tribe sat around the fire in the center of the village. The women pointed to the dark sky and wailed as if they thought the moon had died. Mary knew the moon would come again. It always did. Then she

wondered if that was still true. She had lost her clothes, her shoes, her family, and her home. Maybe she had lost the moon, too.

The old woman Hi-hi-ih placed a large branch on the fire. Its dried leaves burst into flame. The firelight flickered across the faces, like hope fighting fear. Hi-hi-ih leaned on her stick. Years and years of carrying wood and children had bent her back. Then she started to speak. Her words flowed past Mary like the Ohio River. Mary didn't even try to understand what she said. She knew that it was a story. Every night someone told one. Mary hadn't seen any books in the village. There were no written words. There were pictures on the blankets, on the belts, and on the straps the women placed across their foreheads to carry things on their backs.

Hi-hi-ih let the children call out what came next. Everyone knew—except Mary. She watched the fire dance along the logs and thought of her own story. Once upon a time, a baby was born on a ship in the middle of the ocean. A storm blew the ship off its course. The ship sailed south to a beautiful island where flowers bloomed all the time and fruit trees were heavy with fruit. The native people lived on a different island with their own flowers and fruit. And so no one had to fight for anything. They could all live happily ever after in their own place.

Mary put her head down on top of her knees. She wasn't a child anymore. She couldn't believe in fairy stories.

Odankot patted Mary's arm and smiled. Odankot waited for Mary to smile back. But Mary didn't want to be happy. She had to remember her family. If Mary didn't, then who would? *Thomas, Jane, Tom, John, Betsey, Mary, Matthew, Robert.*

In the distance, Mary heard loud whoops and shouts. Branches cracked. Leaves rustled. The shouts got louder. People were coming.

The women and children jumped up excitedly. They all started jabbering. Mary was worried. She had no idea what was going on. With so little light, she couldn't see the expressions on their faces.

Three warriors burst out of the darkness and into the circle. The women shouted. One of the warriors waved a bloody knife. Mary gasped.

The children happily danced. Someone shook

the turtle-shell rattle. Then the oldest woman called. Everyone was silent. She chanted and raised her arms up toward the sky. "Nee-yah-wenh, Ha-wen-ni-yu."

Everyone echoed what she was saying. Mary was shocked. Were they giving thanks for a murder?

A Seneca war chief, born in 1732, who fought in the French and Indian War.
[F. Bartoli]

Then one of the warriors held up a bloody antler. Now Mary understood. The warriors had killed a deer.

The warrior with the bloody antler came over to Jako-ki and Odankot. He pointed the antler at Mary and said something.

Jako-ki answered with many words, including "Dehgewanus."

"Dehgewanus?" the warrior said questioningly. He stared at Mary. Then he spoke sternly for a long time. He looked angry, but Mary didn't know why.

Then Odankot pointed at the warrior. "Kau-jises-tau-ge-au."

Mary guessed that was his name. Three black feathers stood up from his stripe of hair. More feathers pierced his earlobes. He wore a medal around his neck.

Jako-ki pointed to Odankot, Kau-jises-tau-ge-au, and herself. Mary understood that they were brother and sisters. Then Odankot pointed to Jako-ki, Odankot, Kau-jises-tau-ge-au, and Mary. Odankot smiled. Mary didn't. She wasn't their sister.

Kau-jises-tau-ge-au said more words. Then he gestured with his arm and walked away in the forest. Jako-ki and Odankot made Mary follow him. Mary struggled to keep up. She had no idea where they were going or why. All she knew was that she had to follow them to whatever her fate would be. Or did she?

The sky was already turning pink. Mary stood and looked toward the east, where the sun would soon bring its warmth and light. The east was where there were real houses and real dishes. Dresses made of cloth. Bread made of flour. Where she could speak her own language to people like herself. Where she wouldn't be alone.

She walked toward the rose-colored sky. Now she could hear the Ohio River. Where there was a fort called Duquesne.

"Dehgewanus!"

Mary walked toward the river. What was it saying? Had there been a battle? Had the British taken over the fort? She had to go there to find out. What if her brothers were searching for her? She had to return to the fort. How else could she be found?

"Dehgewanus!"

And if the French were still at the fort, then Mary would follow the river until she came to another fort. She wouldn't lose her way. She wouldn't be hungry. Or frightened of the wolves. Or the panthers. Or the warriors.

"Dehgewanus!"

Mary didn't answer. That wasn't her name. She couldn't stay here with the Seneca. But she couldn't go into the wilderness by herself—she was afraid.

When Odankot found her behind the tree, Mary didn't try to run away. She helped the sisters drag Kaujises-tau-ge-au's deer back to the village.

CHAPTER 12

The tall wooden pole that stood near the largest bark house was decorated. One side of the pole had red stripes. The other side had red marks in the shape of crosses. Mary wondered what they meant.

Kau-jises-tau-ge-au showed one mark to Mary. He pointed to it and to her. Mary guessed the mark meant her, but she didn't understand what it said. His stare made her uncomfortable. He rarely smiled, unless Jako-ki teased him or Odankot brought him food.

Days passed. The moon had grown full. The sun was also higher in the sky. Mary didn't have to stay close to the fire for warmth, which was good because she didn't like to be near the warriors. They sat there sharpening the blades of their knives. They cut the deerskin into strips. They used these strips to fasten sharp stones onto their axes.

Now, when her work was done, she went to the bank of a little creek. She sat on a moss-covered rock and listened to the water rush past. Birds sang to her from trees whose tight buds had opened into leaves. Sometimes, as she watched a bee sip from a beautiful flower, she forgot to remember how she had been ripped from her home and most of her family had been killed.

One afternoon, as she sat in her special place, she heard the children calling her.

"Dehgewanus! Ka-jih!"

They wanted her to come.

Mary could now understand more of what was said, even when people didn't speak as patiently as Odankot. Seneca words no longer rushed past Mary like a raging river. Now she could put together enough words to arrive at a meaning.

Jis-ta-ah and Ha-no-wa looked down at her from the top of the bank. Jis-ta-ah was jumping with excitement. Her doll was in a special basket. Ha-no-wa had a basket, too. "Dehgewanus! Ka-jih!"

Mary had learned that *he-eh* meant "no." *Toh-kes* meant "yes." But Mary didn't answer the children with either word. She still hadn't spoken. She didn't think she could ever make such strange sounds come out of her mouth. Besides, there wasn't anything she wanted to say. No one had taught Mary the words for loss or sadness. Or for the cold gray ashes that remained in the pit after the warm fire had been put out.

"Dehgewanus! Ka-jih!" This time Jako-ki called, so Mary went over to them. Jako-ki handed Mary a basket and told her to help. Then she waved Mary off with the children.

They took an unfamiliar path through the woods. Ha-no-wa led the way uphill. Jis-ta-ah danced beside him, but she couldn't make him hurry. His name meant *turtle* for a reason. When they reached a fork in the path, the children argued about which way to go. Jis-ta-ah pointed left. Ha-no-wa chose right. Mary wasn't sure whom to follow. Then she saw that both paths led to the bright green of an open meadow.

"Shes-a-ha!" the children cried.

The children
disappeared into
the tall grass.
After a few
moments, Jis-
ta-ah jumped up and
held out her hands.
They were filled with
wild strawberries.

Mary put one of the tiny
berries in her mouth. She let the sweet juice spread
across her tongue. She hadn't had fresh fruit for months
and months—not since her father had divided up the
last apple into eight sections so that they all could have
a piece. *Thomas, Jane, Tom, John, Betsey, Mary, Matthew,
Robert.*

Mary started to cry.

"Dehgewanus?" Jis-ta-ah sniffed the fruit, wonder-
ing what was wrong with it.

Mary shook her head and smiled. She knelt down
to pick berries, too.

They picked all afternoon. After Mary had filled
her basket, she stared at the mounds of fruit. Here was
food for several days. She should run now while the

children were looking for berries on the ground. Now while the sun was high above the trees. Now while she didn't feel afraid.

Mary faced east toward the river. She would follow it to the fort. She could travel far before the sisters found out she was gone. No one would miss her.

"Dehgewanus!" Jis-ta-ah held up the doll. She talked excitedly about something.

Run, Mary told herself. Her legs were longer than theirs. She could disappear into the woods.

"Dehgewanus!"

Jis-ta-ah sounded so upset, Mary had to hurry over to her. The doll's grass ribbon had come undone. Mary tied a new bow. Then she dipped the tip of another piece of grass into a smushed strawberry and painted a smile on the doll.

When the baskets were full, the children and Mary carried them slowly and solemnly back to the village.

The oldest woman took the berries from Jis-ta-ah and Ha-no-wa. She praised the children and put their berries in a kettle. But when Mary offered her basket, the oldest woman peered into Mary's face. She asked Mary a question. Mary couldn't understand her words. Then the oldest woman said something about

Ha-wen-ni-yu, which was the Seneca's name for the Great Spirit.

Jako-ki argued with the oldest woman. They both said, "Dehgewanus." Mary knew the name meant something different to each one. The oldest woman pushed aside Mary's basket. Mary tried not to care that her berries had been rejected. But she did.

The oldest woman poured water over the mashed berries and added maple sugar. She gave the children a lump of sugar. But she wouldn't let anyone taste the juice.

The next day, the Strawberry Festival began.

Everyone gathered in the center of the village. The sachem peace chief stood up. He was one of the tribe's leaders. Today he wore a special hat decorated with many white and red feathers. He made a long speech. Mary couldn't understand most of it. She heard him say the word *nee-yah-wenh* again and again and point to the berries, to the kettle of juice, to the fire, to the blue sky, to the sun, to the fire. Nee-yah-wenh, nee-yah-wenh, nee-yah-wenh.

Jis-ta-ah sat near Mary. She had the doll with the strawberry smile. She whispered to Mary, "Nee-yah-wenh, Dehgewanus."

Thank you, Mary thought.

The women shook the turtle-shell rattles. Two men led the dance. They stepped with one foot and then patted the ground with the other. They moved one way around the fire, while the rattles kept the beat. Then the men waved their arms like wings. The dance got faster. The women and children joined in. Every so often, someone yelped. The dance got even faster and wilder. Soon everyone was dancing except those shaking the rattles—and Mary, who sat alone.

The dance lasted for an hour. Then the sachem peace chief raised his arm. The drums and chants stopped. He beckoned to Jis-ta-ah and Ha-no-wa. The children carried around the large kettle, offering the juice to each member of the tribe. Before taking a sip from the ladle, everyone said, "Nee-yah-wenh, Ha-wen-ni-yu." Thank you, Great Spirit.

After Odankot had her sip, Jis-ta-ah and Ha-no-wa stood in front of Mary and waited. Mary didn't know what to do. She didn't want to speak. But she didn't dare drink without giving thanks. Mary felt her face flush red. She hated never knowing what to do.

"Dehgewanus shes-a-ha," Jako-ki said.

The Seneca laughed.

Of course, Mary's face was the color of a strawberry. She shook her head, no thank you. She pointed the ladle toward Jako-ki.

The children didn't move. They waited.

"Nee-yah-wenh, Ha-wen-ni-yu," Jis-ta-ah urged, reminding Mary what to say.

Mary's mother had taught her a different prayer. *Our Father, who art in heaven.* That was what she should be praying. *Thy will be done.* What was his will? What should she do? *Forgive us our trespasses as we forgive those who trespass against us.*

Yes, forgive. Mary looked at the faces of Odankot and Jako-ki. Somehow, even after losing their loved one, they had found a way to forgive.

Mary was grateful for that. "Nee. Yah. Wenh," Mary said.

Jis-ta-ah held the ladle to Mary's lips. Mary drank the sweet juice.

"Nee. Yah. Wenh," she said again.

CHAPTER 13

GADE A GU' NA

The Moon When Everything Is Bearing Food

After the strawberries were eaten, the raspberries were ripe. And when they had all been picked, it was time for blueberries. The cornstalks grew taller than Ha-no-wa and Jis-ta-ah. The bean and squash plants had blossoms. It was summer. Every plant was bearing food—even some that Mary didn't know could be eaten.

One day Odankot took Mary into the forest and dug under a leafy plant. She brought up several small lumps of dirt. Mary took one lump in her hand and cleaned it off. It was a tiny potato!

Mary wanted to tell Mama she didn't need to work so hard to grow them in her garden. She could just dig them up from the woods. Then Mary sighed. She couldn't tell Mama anything, not even that sometimes she forgot to say her prayers.

"Come, Dehgewanus. More potatoes here," said Odankot.

The two women knelt side by side and dug in the dirt. Mary found a big lump. She excitedly brushed off the dirt. Unfortunately, it was a rock.

"We would have to cook that a long time." Odankot laughed.

Mary did, too. She was learning to enjoy the way the Seneca teased one another.

"Follow the root. It connects." Odankot brought her hands together to show Mary the meaning of the word.

Mary reached under the leaves and traced the root with her fingers until she found several potatoes. They seemed so small. Should she let the tiny little potatoes stay in the ground until they were bigger? Wasn't it wrong to uproot them before they were ready? Wasn't it cruel to rip them from the mother plant? She didn't have the words to say all that. But she thought for a moment.

"Grow bigger?" Mary said in Seneca.

Odankot smiled, proud that her student had almost made a sentence. "We can come back in half a moon."

Mary replanted the little potatoes. Then she held up the rock. "Plant this?"

They both started to laugh. Then Odankot put her hand on Mary's arm.

Someone was running through the woods.

Was it a deer? A turkey? A rabbit? Small animals made sounds bigger than their size. Mary never knew how much to fear—or hope that this time the one running would be someone to rescue Mary.

It wasn't. It was a warrior Mary didn't recognize. They watched him run past.

Odankot stood up and looked toward the village. "He brings news."

"News?" Mary's heart pounded as if she had been running with the warrior. Had there been a battle? Had the British taken Fort Duquesne?

"Maybe he wants our warriors to go fight Yengeese," Odankot said.

Mary looked down at her moccasins. She sometimes forgot that the Seneca were on the side of the French in the war.

Odankot knelt again. Her loose black hair fell over

her shoulder. She twisted it back and tucked it in her feathered collar. "Let's dig. No matter what the warriors do, we will always need potatoes."

"Why do they have to fight?" Mary said.

"War is their business. Our brother was proud to defend us. But oh, I was sad to see him go," Odankot said.

"Kau-jises-tau-ge-au came back," Mary said.

Odankot shook her head. "Our other brother didn't."

"You had another brother?"

"Yes. He died fighting Yengeese. That is why we adopted Dehgewanus."

Mary remembered when she first arrived. How the women had mourned the death of a hunter. He must have been the brother. "I'm sorry."

Odankot smoothed Mary's hair and fixed the deerskin that tied back the yellow curls. "No, Dehgewanus. Do not be sad. He is in the Blue."

"Blue?"

Odankot pointed to the sky. "With the Great Spirit."

Mary nodded. "Blue." Her own family was also in the Blue.

"Do not be sad," Odankot said again. "Do not think on what we have lost. We have so much. Potatoes."

Mary picked up the rock.

Odankot laughed. But Mary hadn't meant to be funny. She felt like nothing good grew in her garden.

Odankot and Mary returned to the village with a full basket.

Hi-hi-ih and the other old women weren't at the cooking fire. They were sitting with the chiefs and the runner at a fire near the council house. Jako-ki was standing at the edge of the circle.

Mary could hear the voices of the old chiefs, but they were too far away for her to understand what they were saying.

Finally, Jako-ki came back. She poked the fire with a stick. Sparks flew up into the night. "They won't let me talk at the council fire. Only old women who have no teeth."

"What is the news?" Odankot said.

"The Six Nations have signed a treaty with the Yengeese at Easton," Jako-ki said.

"Six Nations?" Mary said.

"Oneida, Onondaga, Mohawk, Cayuga, Tuscarora. And Seneca," Jako-ki said.

"Seneca signed?" Mary couldn't believe what she was hearing. If the Seneca had a treaty with the English, that changed everything.

"Of course. Six Nations must all agree. Tribes do not fight like Yengeese and French," Jako-ki said.

"What does the treaty say?" Odankot asked.

"We must not help the French fight Yengeese," Jako-ki said.

"Then Kau-jises-tau-ge-au will not go to war?" Odankot said.

"No. And Yengeese must stay away from our hunting grounds by the Ohio," Jako-ki said.

"That is good news," Odankot said.

Jako-ki looked at the stick in her hand. "We have had treaties before. We know what Yengeese words are worth." She broke the stick and threw the pieces in the fire.

Mary watched the sticks burn. Had the English broken their promises? Why would they do that? Then she remembered her father always called the tribes savages. He said they didn't deserve the land because they didn't farm or build houses.

Now Mary knew differently. She slept in a bark house. She ate the corn the tribes grew. They had cared for her. But if the Seneca weren't fighting the English anymore, then maybe she could go home.

The last of the corn was harvested. The kernels were ground into hominy. The ears were buried in deep holes and hung from the rafters to dry. The tribe celebrated with a feast to give thanks to the Great Spirit, Ha-wen-ni-yu. The next day, the entire tribe got ready to leave the village of Wiishto. They would travel down the Ohio River to the hunting grounds near Scioto, where they spent each winter.

There was a lot to do to move the whole village. Even the children had to help carry bundles down to the river's edge. Everyone was running back and forth from the village to the river. Then there was a shout. The first canoes had set off.

"This winter I will kill a deer." Ha-no-wa pretended to shoot an arrow.

"Little boys kill little birds," Jis-ta-ah said.

"Little girls grind corn," Ha-no-wa said.

The children were excited, but Mary didn't want to go *down* the Ohio. She wanted to go *up*. The British must be at the fort now. Why else would the tribes sign a treaty with them? Mary clutched a small pouch that hung from a strip of deerskin around her neck. The bit of lace was hidden there.

More canoes set off. One came back. Someone had forgotten a basket. Odankot was helping tie a cradle-board to a woman's back. Jako-ki was arguing with Kau-jises-tau-ge-au about how to load the canoe. Soon they would be leaving. Soon Mary would be taken farther away from the fort.

Then, without really thinking, she walked through the village and past the cornfield. She crossed the little river on a fallen log. She headed north along the Ohio. She would get to Fort Duquesne. What would it be called now that it was British?

Thomas, Jane, Tom, John, Betsey, Mary, Matthew, Robert.

Her heart pounded. It was morning. She hoped to reach the fort by night. She could do it. All

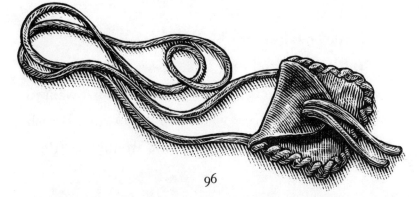

she had to do was follow the Ohio. All she had to do was find the strength to keep running.

Thomas, Jane, Tom, John, Betsey, Mary, Matthew, Robert.

She paused to listen to the river. She wanted to hear it sing its encouragement. But she didn't hear the Ohio. She heard Jako-ki calling to her. "Dehgewanus!"

Mary could hear their paddles digging into the water. They had to fight against the current. Could Mary run faster than they could paddle? No, she couldn't.

"Did you forget something?" Odankot shouted.

Mary sank down behind a dead tree. Maybe she could hide until the sisters gave up and rejoined the rest of the tribe.

"Dehgewanus!" Odankot shouted.

The canoe landed near Mary. She hadn't hidden herself very well. She knew the sisters would never leave her all alone in the forest. They understood how dangerous that would be. They were wiser than she was.

Mary kissed the pouch with the scrap of lace and tucked it back inside her tunic. Then she slowly walked down to the river and got into the sisters' canoe.

CHAPTER 14

Mary was afraid the sisters would be angry that she had tried to run away.

But Odankot said, "Poor Jako-ki had to paddle up-river to look for Dehgewanus. Now her arms are so tired, our canoe will never be faster than Kau-jises-tau-ge-au."

Even the sharp-tongued Jako-ki didn't scold. "Poor Odankot was so worried that Dehgewanus had fallen into the river. Now the sun can come out from the clouds."

Mary had learned this was the Seneca way. They didn't punish those who had done wrong; they tried to comfort those who had suffered. But the sisters didn't know how it hurt Mary's heart to have failed again.

They traveled for three days before they reached the place where the Scioto River joined with the Ohio. They moved their blankets and food into the bark houses that the tribe had left last spring. The hunters went into the woods. After a week, they brought back several doe and a buck. Even Ha-no-wa somehow managed to kill a squirrel. He insisted that it be skinned and cooked, just like the deer.

"We will have to eat squirrel if the Yengeese don't keep their promise," one warrior said.

"I saw boot tracks on our hunting grounds." Another warrior stared at Mary.

"You should hunt elk instead of excuses," Jako-ki said.

The days got colder. The nights got longer. The moon got smaller. And then came the night when it was dead again. Mary had seen nine dead moons since she had come to live with the Seneca. The old women's wails were especially alarming this time, because the sun rose late and set so early. It was the longest night of the year.

In the morning, a tiny sliver appeared, almost impossible to see against the pale winter sky. This was the moon for when the sun was returning. Now the days would get lon-  ger. But spring was still several moons away.

Mary huddled under her blanket as close to the fire as possible. The cold weather made her feel even more alone, as if her spirit had crawled into a cave to sleep. One year ago, Mama had cooked a goose. Betsey and Mary had made three pies. Father decorated the house with pine boughs and red berries. Candles had bright- ened the long, dark nights. They had sung carols. *What child is this, who, laid to rest . . .*

Suddenly, there was a loud knocking on the wall of the bark house.

"They are here!" Odankot cried.

"Quick!" Jako-ki scattered dirt over the fire.

The warm flames were extinguished, and Mary lost even that small comfort.

Warriors rushed into the bark house. Despite the cold, they wore only breechcloths and feathers in their hair. One marched to the fire, scooped up the ashes with a paddle, and swung it around. Clouds of ash floated in every direction.

"Time to get rid of the old," Jako-ki said.

Mary wondered what she meant.

After all the ashes had been taken from the pit, the children brought wood and dried pine needles to make a new fire.

"We begin again!" several people shouted.

The warriors rushed outside. Guns were fired. They knocked on the walls of the next house.

After all the fires had been put out and relit, the tribe gathered in the council house. The drums began. Some took turtle shells and rubbed the walls of the house. Then the dancing began. Mary sat as close to Odankot as possible. Odankot tried to get Mary to dance, too. But Mary shook her head and huddled under her blankets.

At times this world seemed like something Mary

dreamed. The frantic dancing. The haze from the smoky fire. The men wearing bearskins. Or maybe they were bears? Now some dancers wore grotesque masks. At least Mary hoped they were masks and not the faces of ghouls.

The tribe feasted on meat and corn and beans. Everyone ate from the same kettle. Jako-ki had smoothed the knotty part of a branch to make Mary a spoon. "Time for the new, Dehgewanus," Jako-ki said.

"Thank you, Jako-ki." Mary was glad to have her own spoon. Jako-ki had done a good job of smoothing away the splinters. But Mary once had a tin spoon and a fork. What had happened to them? Were they still lying on the floor by the broken table? Or had the Jemisons' house been burned?

"Why is there good? Why is there evil? Why do we live here on this earth?"

The oldest woman started a story. Drums stopped. Everyone sat down to listen.

———————✦◆◆⊂———————

This is how everything began.

Long ago, humans lived in the sky near a tall tree.

There was light when it bloomed. But once its white blossoms fell, there was dark until its flowers opened again.

The chief's daughter became terribly ill. Someone in the tribe dreamed that she would be cured only if the people pulled up the tree. No one wanted to do that. But after the same dream came a third time, the people dug around the tree. When the last root was cut, the tree disappeared into a bottomless hole. The people brought the chief's daughter to where the tree had been, hoping she would be cured. Instead, she too fell into the hole.

The young woman fell through darkness toward the water. There was no land anywhere. The animals looked up and saw her. They decided to save her. The hawk flew up to catch her, and put her on the turtle's back. The turtle couldn't hold her forever. The animals needed land. Several dove into the water. Toad came back with wet dirt. Beaver patted the mud down on Turtle's back to make an island.

After the young woman recovered, she gave birth to a daughter. She raised her daughter on the island, and they ate potatoes that they grew there. Eventually, the daughter became pregnant. She died giving birth to twin brothers.

The older boy was kind and wise, but the younger was always angry. They wanted the island to have more living things. They made forests and lakes together, but each wanted to make his own animals. The older brother made human beings. He made fat, slow animals and sycamore trees with fruit. The younger brother couldn't make humans. This made him so angry, he made giant mosquitoes and ugly animals that ate humans.

The two brothers each went to see what the other had made. The older brother grabbed the giant mosquito and rubbed it until it was tiny. The younger brother wanted life to be hard for the humans. He made the slow animals faster so they couldn't be caught, and the sycamore fruit impossible to eat. He made all the rivers flow downstream so that humans would have to work to travel.

When the brothers saw how each had changed the other's half of the island, they got into a terrible fight. The older brother was killed. He went home to the sky. Those who live good lives go to join him. But the younger brother kept making evil on earth. When evil people die, he torments them. And all because he couldn't make a human.

———◦◦◦———

The celebration continued for three more days. Dreams were told. Meanings were found. There was more feasting and dancing.

Then the old men, several of the warriors, and the old women sat around a separate fire inside the council house.

Mary couldn't hear what they were saying, but she could tell they were disagreeing about something. They all turned to look at Mary. Then they talked again until they nodded and passed around a pipe, each taking a puff and blowing smoke up toward the roof. Someone kicked dirt on that fire. They rejoined the others. The drumming slowed down. Several warriors removed their masks. One by one, people left the council house.

"It's done. The evil is gone from the village," Odankot said.

Mary was glad. But she wondered what they could do to chase it from the rest of the world.

CHAPTER 15

HE SATA
The Moon When Plants Grow Again

After Mary Had Crossed One Winter with the Seneca

The warriors killed plenty of deer, but for some reason, there were no elk. They also trapped many beaver. The pile of pelts was as tall as Jis-ta-ah. The tribe made many plans for what they would get at the trading post. The women wanted a new kettle. The biggest one leaked. They said they wanted to feed stew to the children—not to the fire. The warriors wanted guns. When Jako-ki reminded them that the war with the Yengeese was over, they laughed. The war wouldn't end until all the white people got back in their big canoes and sailed across the ocean.

When the first buds appeared on the bushes, the tribe loaded up the canoes to return to their village at

Wiishto. Ha-no-wa tried to ride on top of pelts, but he was made to sit in the bottom of the canoe.

Paddling against the current was difficult. Melting snow added to the waters of the Ohio. Sometimes the wind was against them, too. The women chanted about the kettles that they wanted. Then the men chanted more loudly about the rifles.

"I don't want kettles or rifles. I want blue beads," Odankot said.

"And little bells so my feet can make music when we dance," Jis-ta-ah said.

"What do you want, Dehgewanus?" Jako-ki said.

"Tea." Mary said the English word without thinking. More than anything, she longed for her mother to make her a cup of tea.

"Do you mean *ti-ti*?" Jako-ki said. That was the Seneca word for "blue jay."

"Yes," Mary said. She still wasn't allowed to speak English.

"You can't get a blue jay at a trading post." Jis-ta-ah laughed.

"Jis-ta-ah is right. We don't need to get blue or music from the white man. The Great Spirit, Ha-wen-ni-yu, has provided us with birds," Odankot said.

At a fork in the river, the canoes with the pelts traveled west toward the trading post. The other canoes continued up the Ohio until they reached the village at Wiishto.

Everyone worked hard. Some unloaded the canoes. Some stored the venison. The bark houses had to be repaired. Mary and the children chased out the mice and the birds that had nested there during the winter.

The women were getting the fields ready for planting when they heard shouts from the river. The other canoes had returned. Everyone rushed to the landing, eager to see what the warriors had brought. Mary was excited, too, even though the days when her father had presents in his pockets seemed like a distant dream.

A pile of pelts was still in the center of each canoe.

"What happened?" Kau-jises-tau-ge-au shouted at the warriors.

"Trading post burned. All dead," they said.

"Burned?" Jako-ki said.

The old women started wailing.

"The French have left Fort Duquesne. Yengeese are there now," the warrior said.

"Yengeese are at the fort?" Mary said excitedly.

Kau-jises-tau-ge-au stared at Mary.

"If we can't trade with the French, how will we get kettles?" the women said.

"We must trade someplace else," Kau-jises-tau-ge-au said.

The canoes were pulled ashore. Two warriors started to unload the pelts.

"Wait. I have an idea." Kau-jises-tau-ge-au glanced at Mary. Then he led the way to the council house. The chiefs and the old women followed him.

Mary's mind jumped around like a grasshopper. If the French were really gone from the fort, she should go. Now. She should run through the forest. If only she could ask the sisters to help her get home.

When evening came, the sachem peace chief covered the council fire with dirt. Kau-jises-tau-ge-au came back to the clan's bark house. He sat by the fire and ate stew.

"Dehgewanus is Yengeese," Kau-jises-tau-ge-au said.

"No. She is Seneca," Jako-ki corrected him.

"Dehgewanus means *two* falling voices," Kau-jises-tau-ge-au said.

"She is our sister. She doesn't speak Yengeese anymore," said Jako-ki.

"But she could. Tomorrow we go to the fort," Kau-jises-tau-ge-au said.

"To Fort Duquesne?" Mary's heart pounded.

"It has a new name now. *Pitt.*" Kau-jises-tau-ge-au practically spit the English name out of his mouth.

Then it was true. The English had taken the fort. "Fort Pitt," Mary said.

"What is Yengeese word for *trade*?" Kau-jises-tau-ge-au asked.

Mary told him the English word.

"You see? She does speak their language. She can help us talk to the Yengeese. Then they will not cheat us," Kau-jises-tau-ge-au said.

"The Yengeese have killed many Seneca. They burned the trading post. Don't take Dehgewanus to talk to them," Jako-ki warned.

"Dehgewanus is *your* sister, too," said Odankot.

"Tomorrow." Kau-jises-tau-ge-au put away his bark bowl.

They all went to bed.

Mary lay in her cot. She smiled in the darkness as she fingered the scrap of lace. *Tomorrow*, she thought. She would go to the fort. Maybe her brothers would be there. Tom and John must have been searching for Mary. They would find her. Tomorrow.

Her head was too full of dreams for sleep. The last one was the worst. She went into the fort. There were so many rooms, she couldn't find her way. Finally, she saw her family. Thomas, Jane, Tom, John, Betsey, Matthew, and Robert were all sitting at a table, eating with spoons. Mary ran to her mother. "I'm here, Mama. I'm here." But Mama pushed her away and shouted, "Go away, you filthy savage!"

Mary woke up. She looked at her hands. Her nails were cracked. Her skin was brown with dirt. She had to go back to the English—before it was too late.

After breakfast, Mary followed Kau-jises-tau-ge-au down to the river. Two canoes piled high with pelts were already in the water. Kau-jises-tau-ge-au dragged another canoe into the water. He held the end steady. As Mary stepped into the center of the canoe, Jako-ki and Odankot ran down the path.

"You can't take Dehgewanus to the fort," cried Odankot.

"She must talk to the Yengeese to make good trades," Kau-jises-tau-ge-au said.

"Then we will go, too," Jako-ki said.

Kau-jises-tau-ge-au frowned, but he let the sisters climb into his canoe.

"I will steer," he said.

"Of course, Brother." Jako-ki bowed and climbed into the front of the canoe. Odankot sat near Mary. Kau-jises-tau-ge-au pushed off from shore and paddled hard.

The Ohio wanted to carry them back downstream toward the village. Mary leaned forward, eager to see the walls of the fort. It took all day before the canoes reached the point of land where two rivers joined to make the Ohio.

The fort seemed bigger than Mary remembered. The British flag flapped in the breeze. Mary tried to see if Tom and John were there. But Kau-jises-tau-ge-au steered the canoe past the fort. They landed on the opposite bank.

The sisters gathered wood and started a fire. "Eat first. Or your stomachs will be talking to the Yengeese," Jako-ki said.

Kau-jises-tau-ge-au laughed.

Odankot ground corn and made mush. Then she patted the mush into cakes and put them in the ashes to bake.

"Why are you making bread?" Mary paced back and forth.

"Dehgewanus likes bread better than stew." Odankot smiled.

That was true. But now Mary stared at the walls of the fort. Were her brothers inside, drinking tea and eating brown bread?

Someone fired a gun.

Kau-jises-tau-ge-au jumped up and grabbed his gun.

No one came outside the fort. No one fired again, but they were all uneasy.

"The Yengeese still think we are enemies," one of the warriors muttered.

"The Treaty of Easton says we won't attack the fort," Kau-jises-tau-ge-au said.

"We keep our promises. Will they?" another warrior said.

Kau-jises-tau-ge-au scooped up a handful of rocks. He tossed them in his hand. Then he let them fall to the ground. He picked up the belt of wampum. Its purple and white shells glistened in the sun. "Come, Dehgewanus. We will eat later."

Mary jumped up and ran over to the canoes. Jako-ki hurried after her. Odankot pushed more ashes over the cakes and then followed.

Two canoes crossed the Ohio. Mary took her yellow hair out of the deerskin tie. With water from the icy river, she tried to scrub her arms, but she only made streaks in the dirt.

Kau-jises-tau-ge-au paddled slowly, searching for a good place to come ashore. "Tell them we want good value for good pelts. Tell them not to cheat," he said.

"Don't be frightened, Dehgewanus," Jako-ki said.

"Our brother won't let them hurt you," Odankot said.

The English weren't going to hurt Mary. They were going to save her! Her heart raced. She felt too excited to speak.

The canoe slid up onto a sandy spot. Jako-ki and

The Iroquois in 1722, examining European goods acquired through trade. [*Bacqueville de La Potherie*, Histoire de l'Amérique septentrionale: divisée en quatre tomes]

Odankot got out of the canoe first. Mary followed. Her legs were wobbly from kneeling in the canoe. She wasn't sure what to do. Should she run around the fort to the entrance? What if the English didn't let her in?

Kau-jises-tau-ge-au held the wampum above his head. "Yengeese!" he shouted.

Two men came around the corner of the fort. They wore blue jackets with shiny buttons. One had a bushy beard. The other had a round belly. They weren't Tom or John.

"What do you want?" the bearded man said in English.

Mary was so happy to hear those crisp sounds again. She stepped in front of the sisters.

"My word. Is that a white girl?" the bearded man said.

"She's probably a French half-breed," the round man said.

"I was kidnapped!" Mary struggled to remember the date. "On April 5th, 1758."

"Good gracious. Today is May 1st, 1759. How did you survive an entire year with these savages?" the round one said.

Jako-ki glared at the men. Odankot looked upset. They might not know the English words, but they understood what the men meant.

"My name is Mary Jemison. My brothers are looking for me. Tom and John Jemison," Mary said.

"Have you heard about a kidnapped Jemison?" the bearded man said.

"No," the round man said.

"No?" Mary cried. Tom and John had to be searching for her. They had to be.

"Yengeese. Easton. Trade," Kau-jises-tau-ge-au said.

The bearded man said to the round man, "What should we do with her?"

"Strip off those filthy clothes and give her a bath," the round man said.

Mary rubbed the tears off her face. She looked at her hands. It was like her dream. Mary needed to explain. But her thoughts swam inside her head.

The bearded man stepped toward Mary. "You better come with us."

Kau-jises-tau-ge-au pulled Mary back. "Trade!"

"You want us to give you something for the girl?" the bearded man said.

"Teh-ya-kwa-teh-neh-tey!" Jako-ki shouted, and pushed the men away.

"No!" Mary said. She wasn't Jako-ki's sister. She called her brothers. "Tom! John!" But Tom and John hadn't come. Tom and John weren't searching for her. There were just these men. They called her filthy. What would they do? Where would they take her? "He-eh. No." Mary's words were so mixed up. She grew dizzy. She felt herself sinking down and down and down.

Odankot rushed to her side.

Odankot and Jako-ki carried Mary back to the river.

"Wait," the round man said.

"Trade!" Kau-jises-tau-ge-au said.

"Teh-ya-kwa-teh-neh-tey!" Jako-ki shouted.

Odankot and Jako-ki put Mary in the canoe. They got in and pushed off from the land with their paddles. The current caught the canoe and carried it away.

CHAPTER 16

The river was fast, but the sisters wanted to go even faster. They paddled hard and sang. *He-ya he ya he yo ho-wi-ne.*

Mary didn't know what the words meant. She didn't care. She let the river take her. It was much stronger than she was. So were the sisters.

He-ya he ya he yo ho-wi-ne.

Suddenly, Odankot cried out, "We left the corn cakes in the fire!"

"Kau-jises-tau-ge-au will eat them," Jako-ki said.

"Good thing he likes them burned," said Odankot.

They paddled in silence for a while. Then Jako-ki said, "You're lucky we were there, Dehgewanus."

Mary felt weak and confused, but she didn't feel lucky.

"Those wicked Yengeese would have kidnapped you," Jako-ki said.

"Wicked?" said Mary.

"One had fur on his face. Who could see what his smile was like?" Odankot said.

"And one was so fat, he must be a cannibal," Jako-ki stated.

"They must have killed many men to get all those medals on their jackets," Odankot said.

Mary didn't even try to explain what buttons were. She twisted the scrap of lace until the threads tore. "What's the matter with me?" she said in English.

"He-eh Yengeese," Jako-ki said.

"He-eh Yengeese," Mary echoed. No English. She had missed her chance to return. No fork, no spoon, no tea, no brown bread, no white aprons, no Father, Mama, Betsey, Matthew, Robert. And no Tom or John, who weren't looking for her after all.

Odankot turned to look behind her at Mary. "Dehgewanus?"

"Paddle, Odankot," Jako-ki said.

So the sisters paddled and sang the song again. *He-ya he ya he yo ho-wi-ne.*

When they reached the little river at Wiishto, Jako-ki expertly steered the canoe around the point and paddled up to the sandy beach. The children ran to greet them.

"Did you see the fort? Is it bigger than the council house?" Jis-ta-ah asked.

"Did you see the Yengeese? Is it true they have furry faces?" Ha-no-wa wanted to know.

"We missed you." Jis-ta-ah made the corn-husk doll dance for Mary.

Mary got out of the canoe and walked quickly into the forest. She heard the children say, "What is wrong with Dehgewanus?"

"Nothing," Jako-ki said.

Jako-ki was right. There was nothing wrong with Dehgewanus. It was Mary who stumbled through the woods until she came to her special place by the little creek. Then she burst into tears. She tried to wipe her eyes on her tunic, but deerskin didn't dry her tears like Mama's apron.

One year ago, Jako-ki had thrown Mary's clothes

into the river. Today, Mary had let the sisters and the river bring her back again. So here she was.

The next day, Mary went to the fields where the women were planting. Mary was supposed to keep the children out of mischief, but her eyes had turned inward. She couldn't see the boys playing in the river. She couldn't see the girls picking poisonous leaves. So Jako-ki gave Mary a short hoe. Mary joined the line of women who were digging holes for the seeds.

The women sang and chattered. Their voices flowed around Mary as if she was a rock in the river. Mary worked hard. When they reached the edge of the field, Mary felt good to look back and see what she had done.

The women crossed the field once more. They put seeds in the holes and covered them with a small mound of dirt.

"Dehgewanus works hard." Odankot smiled at her.

Mary sighed. Yes, Dehgewanus worked hard. But Mary was walking in her sleep.

Another moon passed. The rain fell. The sun shone. The seeds sent their roots into the soil. The leafy stems grew up toward the light. The women returned to the field to pull the weeds that were crowding out the young crop.

Jako-ki showed Mary the kinds of plants they wanted to grow. Mary didn't listen. She was eager to get to work. She pulled lots of weeds and tossed them aside.

The line of women crossed the field, chattering and laughing as always. Even though Mary understood what they were saying, she didn't know how to shake the sadness that clung to her like cobwebs.

"Stop, Dehgewanus, what are you doing?" Jako-ki scolded her.

All the women gathered around. Jako-ki picked up one of the plants that Mary had pulled. "These aren't weeds."

Mary pointed to the corn. "This is corn. This is a weed."

"No, it's bean."

Odankot took the limp plant Mary had tossed aside and carefully put it back into the soil next to the corn.

"Why are you planting beans in the cornfield?" Mary's father planted corn with corn. That was the correct way.

"Three sisters help one another grow," Odankot said.

Mary shook her head vehemently. "Corn should be with corn. Beans with beans."

"Dehgewanus is still learning our ways." Odankot's brown eyes looked sadly at Mary.

Her pity made Mary angrier. She threw down the hoe. "Of course I don't know your ways. I'm white. So why didn't you let me stay with the whites at the fort?"

All the native women stared. They were shocked to hear Mary talk like this.

"We told you why. Those Yengeese were wicked. They said bad things about you. They wanted to take you away from us. Even though we adopted you. We looked after you. We helped you cross a winter," Jakoki said.

"I should be with Yengeese," Mary said.

"You didn't know them. They're strangers. Where would they take you? What would they do to you?

Make you their slave? We had to protect you," Jako-ki said.

Odankot took Mary's hand. "You're our sister."

Their kindness toward her made Mary feel ashamed. "But I'm not like you."

"Corn, bean, squash," Jako-ki said.

"Three sisters," said Odankot.

"What do you mean?" Mary asked.

"They help one another grow. The cornstalk lifts the beans up from the dirt. The squash spreads across the ground and keeps new weeds from growing," Jako-ki said.

"What good is the bean? How does the bean help the other sisters?" asked Mary.

"The Great Spirit, Ha-wen-ni-yu, knows. He gave us all three: We call them *dio-heh-ko* because they sustain us." Odankot said.

"Dio-heh-ko. Three sisters grow best together," said Jako-ki.

Mary thought about this for a moment. She knelt down to put a bean plant back into the ground. Now it could be nourished by the soil. And when the rains came, it could hang on to the earth and not get washed away.

CHAPTER 17

GADE' A

The Moon When Food Begins to Form

The cornstalks grew tall and straight. The beans climbed up around the stalks. The squash plants spread across the ground. What had seemed like barren soil was lush with life. Yellow blossoms became tiny squash. Ears of corn began to form beside the little beans. These miracles happened every year in fields all over the world. But this year Mary felt particularly proud of how the three crops grew together—and grateful that they did.

After another moon passed, the first kernels formed on the ears. It was time for the Green Corn Festival.

The warriors went off to hunt so that there would be fresh meat for the feast. The women began preparing the food. Jako-ki gave Mary the jawbone of a deer and an ear of corn with tiny tender kernels. "Scrape off the kernels with this."

"Make sure you save the sweet juice," Odankot said.

"The deer chews the corn first," Ha-no-wa said. He took the cob Mary had scraped and sucked it.

"Ha-no-wa chews it last," Jis-ta-ah said.

The old woman Hi-hi-ih got out the new kettle that Kau-jises-tau-ge-au had gotten for the pelts at Fort Pitt. Mary put some of the juicy kernels she had scraped into the kettle. Jako-ki took the rest and added green beans, berries, chopped apples, and dried meat. Then they wrapped this mixture in several corn leaves. Each packet was tied with a string of bark and put in another kettle full of boiling water.

"I'm hungry already. When will the hunters return?" Ha-no-wa said.

"Someone else is hungry for the hunters," Odankot teased.

Jako-ki tossed one of her braids over her shoulder. "Dehgewanus?"

"What? I'm not hungry for hunters." Mary put a handful of dried corn into a hollowed-out log. She picked up her wooden corn pounder to grind the kernels with the heavy end of the stick.

"Jako-ki is teasing. She's the one who has been practicing the wedding dance. She's tired of two braids." Odankot pulled one of Jako-ki's braids.

"Jako-ki wants a husband? She better find someone who is deaf," Mary said.

"Or someone from a distant clan who never heard her sharp tongue," Odankot said.

"I have no time for a husband," Jako-ki said. "Who would look after you and Dehgewanus?"

"I will! I will bring you so much meat, your bellies

will drag on the ground." Ha-no-wa took the stick he used for a bow and shot many imaginary arrows. Then he danced and whooped to celebrate his successful hunting.

Everyone laughed—until they heard answering whoops from the forest.

No one recognized the voices. The women stood up to see who was coming. Jis-ta-ah hid behind Mary. Ha-no-wa raised his imaginary bow. Then Jako-ki brought him behind her.

Six warriors came toward the village. They had tattoos inked across their faces. They wore capes made of turkey feathers. One had a small square of scarlet deerskin hanging from his neck. He spoke first. "Lenape greet our Seneca cousins. My name is Sheninjee."

"You are welcome, Sheninjee," the oldest woman said. "You're just in time for the Green Corn Festival."

The warriors sat by the fire. They smiled at the rows of corn roasting in the coals.

"How do you celebrate your Green Corn Festival?" Sheninjee said.

"We give thanks and dance and feast," Hi-hi-ih said.

"We used to do that, too," Sheninjee said.

"Why don't you anymore?" asked Jako-ki.

"We can't plant corn if we have no land," Sheninjee replied.

The Lenape warriors looked at Mary. Mary bent her head and tried to keep pounding the corn. The men made her so nervous that she crushed her finger between the pounder and the edge of the log. It hurt, but she bit her lip to keep from crying out. She didn't want them to know how they worried her.

Now that a year had passed, none of the Seneca stared at Mary anymore. Her sisters teased her whenever her face was the color of a strawberry. The children still liked to play with her hair. The tribe had accepted her. But she guessed from the strangers' words that they had plenty of reason not to like the Yengeese.

"After the feast, we have gambling games," Jako-ki said.

"What will you bet?" Sheninjee asked.

"Something precious," Jako-ki responded.

"How about your tongue? Then we could enjoy silence," said Odankot.

Everybody laughed.

The sun had set when Kau-jises-tau-ge-au and the other Seneca warriors came into camp. They shouted with triumph about how many deer they had killed.

The women went into the woods to drag the game to the village. Mary followed her sisters. She was glad to get away from the Lenape's eyes.

"I will bet my beaded necklace. What will you bet, Dehgewanus?" Odankot said.

"I have nothing of my own," Mary said as she fingered the small pouch she wore around her neck that contained the scrap of lace.

"You have your corn pounder," Jako-ki said.

"I shall bet that. Whoever wins it will have to pound my corn," Mary said.

Their laughter was cut short when they found the deer the warriors had killed.

They said thanks to the Great Spirit. They tied the deer's body to three long branches with strings of elm bark and dragged it back to the village.

"Did you see the marks on Sheninjee's forehead?" Odankot said.

"Three snakes and one spear," Mary said.

"I have heard the Lenape marks show what they have done," Jako-ki said.

"Sheninjee killed three snakes with one spear?" Odankot asked.

But Mary knew that snakes were also symbols for traitorous men. She wondered how many of those he had killed—and if they were Yengeese.

After the deer was skinned, its meat was added to the stew pots. While the food cooked, the tribe sat around the fire with the Lenape.

"Have the Seneca made a treaty with the Yengeese?" Sheninjee inquired.

"Yes," Kau-jises-tau-ge-au said.

"They gave you wampum?" asked Sheninjee.

"And kettles and guns!" Ha-no-wa said.

"They also promised to stay away from our Ohio valley," the sachem peace chief said.

"If they don't, we will fight them again," a warrior claimed.

"No more war. We will keep our promise. We won't help the French fight Yengeese. And they will let us live here in peace," Kau-jises-tau-ge-au stated.

"Did you make that promise by marking their paper?" Sheninjee shook his head.

"That is how the Yengeese make treaties," the warrior chief said.

"Then you don't know what you agreed to," replied Sheninjee.

"The Yengeese told us," Kau-jises-tau-ge-au said.

"They also told us. But their marks on paper are like footprints in the snow." Sheninjee took out a beautiful stone pipe and lit it. "Have you heard of the Walking Purchase treaty?"

Jako-ki put more wood on the fire. The children settled on Mary's lap to listen.

"William Penn was an honorable Yengeese," Sheninjee said.

Mary remembered her father had brought his family to Pennsylvania because they could worship as they wished in William Penn's colony.

"The Lenape had peace with him. But he died more than forty winters ago. His sons were not like their father. They said the Lenape had signed a treaty selling Yengeese some of our land along the Delaware River," Sheninjee said.

"How much?" Kau-jises-tau-ge-au asked.

"As much as a man could walk in a day and a half," said Sheninjee.

"That is not so much. If the path wanders through forests. And if the man is not a deer," Kau-jises-tau-ge-au said.

Sheninjee blew smoke from his pipe. "And if the man is not Yengeese."

He said that word so coldly that Mary drew the children closer to her.

"But they were," the sachem peace chief said.

"They were. Before the day of the walking, many Yengeese went into the forest. They cleared brush to make a wide trail," Sheninjee said.

"That's not fair," Mary said.

Sheninjee stared at Mary. She couldn't read his expression. The firelight flickered across the snakes drawn on his face.

"The Yengeese promised their fastest runners rewards for whoever could win. They ran and ran and ran on the wide trail."

"You said they were supposed to walk," Kau-jises-tau-ge-au said.

"They were. But they didn't. When the day and a half of running was done, all the land along the Delaware River had been stolen away."

There was silence. The wind stirred the leaves of the trees.

"And so we thank you, Seneca cousins, for inviting us to your Green Corn Festival. We're grateful to eat the corn we have no place to grow," Sheninjee said.

Hi-hi-ih filled bark bowls with stew and gave them to the Lenape. The oldest woman chanted the thanks to the Great Spirit.

His story told, Sheninjee silently ate his food.

But he didn't take his black eyes off Mary.

CHAPTER 18

After the Green Corn Festival feast, Kau-jises-tau-ge-au did the stomp-step to start the Great Feather Dance. "Hyo," he said.

"Yo hee," the tribe answered.

Hyo, yo hee. Hyo, yo hee.

Odankot jumped up. She was always eager to dance. One by one, the rest of the Seneca followed Kau-jises-tau-ge-au. The line of dancers snaked counterclockwise around the fire.

Hyo, yo hee. Hyo, yo hee.

Ha-no-wa proudly shook the turtle-shell rattle and tried to keep the turkey feathers from falling out of his hair. Two old chiefs beat the drums.

When Mary had first heard native drums, they only sounded loud. But now she could tell they had different pitches.

Hyo, yo hee. Hyo, yo hee.

Mary's toes tapped inside her moccasins as people danced past. Odankot looked so beautiful as she waved her arms. Even Jako-ki had a peaceful smile. Mary wondered how it would feel to move as one with the tribe. But she wasn't sure she could, or that she should. It was a Seneca dance.

Hyo, yo hee. Hyo, yo hee.

Now even the oldest women were dancing. Only two people still sat on opposite sides of the fire. The line of dancers passed between them, but Mary felt Sheninjee's stare. What was he thinking?

She didn't need to wonder. She knew. His eyes smoldered like a fire so hot nothing could extinguish it. He hated her because she was white. Whites had cheated Lenape out of their land. Mary's father had made his farm on stolen acres. Even if the land hadn't belonged to the Lenape, it had been used by other tribes—and deer and elk and rabbits and eagles and owls.

As Odankot danced past, she smiled and tried to pull Mary into the line.

Mary was amazed that these sisters had embraced her. They had just as much reason to hate whites as Sheninjee did. Their brother had been killed in the French and Indian War. But somehow they had made a home for Mary in their hearts.

"Dance, Dehgewanus." Jako-ki deliberately did the stomp-step on Mary's moccasin.

Mary laughed, and shook her head.

Sheninjee frowned as he said, "Dehgewanus?"

Now he knew her name. Mary's face flushed red as a strawberry.

He stared as if he had never seen this happen to anyone before.

She jumped up to run from his eyes. Jako-ki pulled her into the line of dancers. Mary did the stomp-step. "Dehgewanus has feet!" Jako-ki cried.

The Seneca laughed with Mary. Then she bit her lip. The line snaked past where Sheninjee still sat. She had to dance near him. Stomp-step, stomp-step. *Hyo, yo hee. Hyo, yo hee.* Closer and closer. He watched her, as if waiting for her to make a mistake. But she lifted her chin proudly and danced past him. She let out her breath with relief.

Then he stood and joined the dance directly behind Mary.

He was much taller than she was. His step made the ground shake. Or maybe fear made her tremble?

She started to lose her balance, but a strong hand grabbed her arm and pulled her back to her feet. Now they were face-to-face.

She wrenched free of his grip and ran away from the fire circle.

She hurried to her cot in the bark house. She lay there listening to the dancing. *Hyo, yo hee. Hyo, yo hee.*

Someone came in. Mary hid under the blanket.

It was Odankot. "Dehgewanus? Are you all right?"

Mary didn't know how to answer that question. She pretended to be asleep.

———⬥———

The next morning, Mary joined the women at the cooking fire. The men were gone. Mary hoped they were hunting deep in the forest. She never wanted to feel Sheninjee's eyes burn her again.

"Ah, Dehgewanus," Hi-hi-ih said. "Did you dream well?"

The Seneca always shared their dreams. They believed dreams were messages from the Great Spirit. This morning the women seemed particularly interested in Mary's.

"Did you dream of a bear?" a woman asked.

"A very, very tall bear?" another woman added.

"I don't think so," said Mary.

"You should ask the bear if he dreamed of Dehgewanus," Jako-ki said.

The women laughed so much that Mary blushed. She thought she had learned the ways of the Seneca. But now she felt ignorant again.

Ha-no-wa ran up the path from the river. His legs were wet. He carried a basket full of fish. The silver tails flashed in the sunlight.

"Look what the Lenape have caught!" he said.

The Lenape warriors came up the path. They were dripping wet. Two of them carried a big net. One carried another basket of fish. Sheninjee wasn't with them.

"Thank you. We will eat well today," Hi-hi-ih said as she took the fish.

Mary and the sisters went to get more wood for the fire.

"Look," Jako-ki whispered.

Kau-jises-tau-ge-au and Sheninjee stood next to the tall red-striped pole.

Sheninjee reached into his pouch and took out a sharp knife. He gave it to Kau-jises-tau-ge-au. Kau-jises-tau-ge-au examined the knife very carefully. Then he nodded and stuck the knife in his belt. Sheninjee reached into his pouch again. This time he took out the pipe carved from stone. Kau-jises-tau-ge-au smiled broadly as he took the pipe. His index finger stroked the smooth stone bowl. He sucked the mouthpiece. He nodded.

"Our brother has always wanted a fine pipe," Odankot said.

"Sheninjee is lucky he had something our brother wanted," said Jako-ki.

"Did Kau-jises-tau-ge-au win those gifts in the gambling game?" asked Mary.

"Sheninjee wins," Jako-ki said.

"How?" asked Mary.

Odankot smoothed Mary's hair into the deer-skin tie.

Sheninjee reached into his pouch a third time. He took out a cape made from the skin of a turkey. He shook it gently. The feathers gleamed in the morning light. Then he held out the cape and slowly walked toward Mary.

Now Mary understood. Kau-jises-tau-ge-au had sold her to Sheninjee. She clung to Jako-ki's arms. "Don't let the Lenape take me away. Please don't let him buy me."

Odankot stroked Mary's hair. "But, Dehgewanus, Sheninjee wants you to be his wife."

CHAPTER 19

"His wife?" Mary wasn't sure she understood the word. She hardly ever heard it.

Sheninjee held out the cape again and waited for Mary to come to him. "I want my wife to be beautiful."

His eyes glowed warmly as he said those words. But Mary was too shocked to respond in any way.

Kau-jises-tau-ge-au motioned impatiently to Mary.

Mary had to do as her brother wished. She left the comfort of her sisters and slowly walked toward the men. She bowed her head so that Sheninjee could place the cape over her shoulders. The feathers were even more beautiful close up. She tried to stand tall, but she felt crushed by its weight.

"Why doesn't she speak? Doesn't she know how?" Sheninjee asked.

"Of course she knows," Kau-jises-tau-ge-au said.

Mary didn't. She had no idea how to express the storm of emotions inside her—not even in English.

She ran away from them, along the path through the forest. She came out in the field where the strawberries grew. It was summer. The sweet berries weren't there. She took off the cape and sat on the grass.

Suddenly, she missed her mother. It often happened that way, like a sharp pain in her side, as if she had run too far or too fast. Mama would have been able to explain to her why strawberries had their season. And why a girl must grow to be a woman.

"Mama?" Mary took the lace out of its pouch. She held it in her palm. It had never been a very large scrap. It was getting smaller all the time. She tried to think of what her mother would want her to do. Her mother had told her to live. But she hadn't said *how*. She couldn't possibly want Mary to take a warrior for her husband.

Mary could love her Seneca sisters. They had never been to war. They had never killed white people. Could Mary live with a man who had?

Someone was coming. Mary jumped up to hide, but it was only Odankot and Jako-ki who came out of the forest shadows.

"The bird tried to fly away?" Jako-ki pointed to the feathered cape.

"It's too heavy," Mary said.

"Sheninjee sent us to ask if you are ill," said Jako-ki.

Mary shook her head.

"But you are sad?" Odankot knelt beside her.

The sisters were as kind to her as if they all had the same mother. But their mother was named Hi-hi-ih. Mary's mother was named Jane.

"I don't want a husband," Mary said.

"Sheninjee is a good man," Odankot said.

"A *tall* man," Jako-ki added.

"He's traveled a long way. That makes a man wise," said Odankot.

"Our brother would not make a bad choice for his sister," Jako-ki stated.

"I know," Mary said.

"Then why don't you like Sheninjee?" asked Jako-ki.

Mary brushed bits of grass off her tunic. "He is Lenape."

"That's all right. Lenape are our cousins," Jako-ki said.

"But I am *not* Lenape," Mary said.

"That's good. Seneca must marry outside their clan," said Jako-ki.

"I'm not Seneca," Mary said.

"You're our sister. We adopted you." Odankot grabbed Mary's hand.

Mary looked at the two hands. The fingers intertwined weren't exactly the same color. That shouldn't matter. That didn't matter. Odankot was good and strong. She never complained. She had a smile like the sun. But Mary couldn't be Odankot's wife.

"Dehgewanus, what's the matter?" Odankot asked, stroking Mary's hand.

"Don't be afraid. Tell us," Jako-ki said.

"How can I go with him?" Mary cried.

Odankot looked at Jako-ki.

"How?" Jako-ki gestured to the field and the forest all around. "That is how life continues. Nothing survives alone. Someday Odankot and I will find husbands."

"If you learn to soften your tongue." Odankot laughed.

Jako-ki stuck out her tongue at her sister.

"I want to stay with you," Mary said.

"You will," replied Jako-ki. "The husband joins the wife's clan and moves into her bark house."

"The husband follows the wife?" Mary was shocked.

"Were you worried that Sheninjee would take you away?" Odankot asked.

"Do Yengeese wives leave their sisters?" Now it was Jako-ki's turn to be shocked.

Mary nodded.

"But that's terrible," Odankot gasped.

"Luckily, you are Seneca now," Jako-ki said.

She pulled Mary up from the field. She brushed the dirt off Mary's tunic. Odankot picked up the bird cape. She put it over Mary's shoulders. Then they all walked back to the village.

Yes, Mary thought. Like it or not, she was Seneca now.

CHAPTER 20

The sisters walked through the forest. Mary stopped to take a stone out of her moccasin. Then she found some wild potatoes to dig. Then there was another stone, in the other moccasin. Finally, Jako-ki said, "It will be winter before we return to the village."

"I'm sorry," Mary said.

"You can't stop plants from growing. They must blossom when it's their time." Odankot led Mary toward the village.

Mary sighed. She didn't feel like it was her time. She felt like she was in a canoe rushing toward a waterfall. She knew there would be a drop. She could see that the river disappeared from sight. She just didn't know how far she would fall. Or how many sharp rocks would be waiting for her at the bottom.

When they reached the cooking fire, the women were all grinning. Even the babies in their cradleboards seemed to know what was about to happen.

"Now Dehgewanus makes the marriage bread," Hi-hi-ih said.

"Take care. If you burn it, he will change his mind," someone said.

Mary considered this while she ground the corn. She wasn't very good at knowing when to take out the bread. Maybe she should burn it. But that might make him angry. Her hand trembled. The corn pounder knocked against the side of the hollow log. Corn spilled out onto the dirt.

"Let me help," said Odankot.

"The wife must make the bread herself," Hi-hi-ih said.

Mary got another handful of corn and started over. This time she concentrated on what she was doing. She ground the corn. She made the mush. She made the bread. She put it on a flat rock at the edge of the fire. When the bread was done, she put it in a special basket. She carried it to the place at the edge of the village where the Lenape had made a rough shelter for themselves out of logs and branches.

Sheninjee sat by a small fire, fixing the feathers on his arrows.

Mary put down the basket. "I have brought the bread."

Sheninjee took a piece of the bread with his left hand and ate it. But he kept hold of the arrow. He stared at her. The Seneca all had dark eyes, so unlike the blue of Mary's family. But Sheninjee's eyes were particularly black and brooding. "Sit," he said.

Mary sat.

He stared at her moccasins. Did he know that she got them the same day she lost her family?

He pointed to the places where the deerskin had worn thin. Then he lifted up his foot so that she could see the patches on the bottom of his deerskin boot.

"We are both far from home," he said.

Mary was surprised at how wistful he sounded. "Yes. We are."

"We can never return."

Mary knew quite well that her old life was gone.

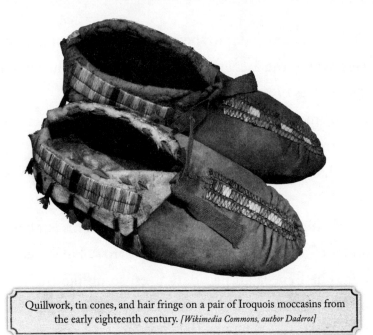

Quillwork, tin cones, and hair fringe on a pair of Iroquois moccasins from the early eighteenth century. *[Wikimedia Commons, author Daderot]*

Even the scrap of lace she kept wasn't much more than a dirty tangle of thread.

"I have spent my life fighting." He fingered the sharp tip of the arrow. "But each wound I make doesn't heal my own wounds."

Mary nodded slowly. "Tears on my cheeks don't heal mine."

Sheninjee put down the arrow. "A wise man is willing to try new ways. A wise man hopes to learn. I asked your brother, how could he have a white woman in his family? He said you weren't a white woman. You were his sister Dehgewanus."

He touched her hair and twisted a yellow lock around his finger. "But you *are* white. We are strangers to each other."

"A wise woman hopes to learn." Mary tried to focus on his eyes. The brown seemed more kindly now. But on his forehead, just an inch away, were the tattoos. Three snakes and one spear. Could she ever look at this man without thinking of the people he had killed?

He seemed to understand what she was thinking. "We must try not to think about the past," he said.

"Or worry about the future," she said.

"A wise man and a wise woman can only try to be happy in the present," he said.

"Yes." Mary agreed. But how? She had lived so long with sadness and fear.

They sat there in silence. A small white butterfly fluttered past them, toward the creek. Then Mary remembered she always felt better when she sat on the moss-covered stone by the creek. Should she take him to her favorite spot? Would he follow her? She looked up at him shyly. "There is a place that brings me peace."

"Show me," he said.

She led the way through the woods and down the ravine. She walked on the log to cross the creek. His legs were so long, he leapt over the little stream. She sat on the moss-covered stone. He crossed his legs and sat at her feet.

In the branches above their heads, a blackbird sang.

"Jako-ki has followed us." Mary pointed to the bird that shared her sister's name.

He laughed so loudly, the bird flew away.

There was silence again. Mary wished Jako-ki was there; she always had something to say. Mary leaned over and dipped her hand in the stream. Water trailed from her fingers.

"Is it true that white people live crowded with strangers? Where the paths have been covered with rocks?" Sheninjee said.

Mary thought for a moment. That was what a city was. "Some do. We lived on a farm." Then she worried if he would ask her where that farm was. Would he ask her how her father got that land?

He looked around at the white birch trees and the sparkling brook. "Did you have a place like this there?"

"No. Nothing so beautiful as this."

He reached past her and picked a small yellow flower. He placed it in her hair.

"Now you must give me something," he said.

"What can I give a warrior?" She showed him her empty hands.

He took her hands. His skin was hard and rough, but his hands were warm. He pulled her closer to him. The bank where he sat was slippery. They toppled into the stream. He tried to lift her out of the water, but they laughed so much, they fell back in again. Then they sat side by side and let the current pass over them. The stream carried away the dust from their journeys. It felt good to be washed clean.

They sat in the water for such a long time that the skin of her hands became wrinkled. She climbed out and sat on the bank. She laughed and showed him her fingers. "Look, Sheninjee. We've grown old together."

"I'm glad to spend my life with you, Dehgewanus," he said.

CHAPTER 21

The sun crossed the sky. Sheninjee and Mary stayed beside the brook. By the time Mary followed Sheninjee back to the village, their clothes were dry.

They stood by the council fire. When the tribe had gathered, Sheninjee and Mary did the step-pat dance together across the room.

"Now you are husband and wife," Kau-jises-tauge-au said. He offered the other warriors a smoke from his new pipe.

"No." The oldest woman pointed at Mary. "Dehgewanus can't marry in the traditional Seneca way. She can't place her braids over Sheninjee. She has bad hair."

Mary tucked her hair behind her ears. It was true.

She had no braids. Her hair never grew much past her shoulders and it was too curly to be bound that way. She looked at Sheninjee. Would he change his mind?

Sheninjee didn't know what to do. He was a stranger to the tribe. He had to respect the oldest woman and the Seneca customs.

Maybe it's for the best, Mary thought. After all, just that morning she had run away from a husband. But the time she spent with him today had changed that. She hadn't known how lonely she was until she wasn't lonely anymore.

She bowed to the oldest woman to show respect. Then she said, "I do not have braids. But I hope I can find another way to claim my husband."

Mary stood in front of Sheninjee.

Sheninjee smiled at Mary. "A wise woman can."

Mary raised her arms and stood on tiptoe to place her hands on his shoulders.

"It is done!" people cheered.

"Now they *are* married," Jako-ki declared.

Kau-jises-tau-ge-au put a new wall inside the elm bark house to make a room for Sheninjee and Mary.

A variation of Iroquois longhouse.
[Wilbur F. Gordy, Stories of American History]

The corn grew taller. The beans were picked. The red leaves fell to the ground. Mary and Sheninjee spent many hours by the little stream. The sun didn't climb as high in the sky. But as long as they were together, they didn't feel the cold.

The squash was picked. The corn was dark red. The women were very busy storing food. Everyone knew that the lovely days of summer couldn't last.

"Look at Dehgewanus!" Jako-ki shouted one day.

Mary rubbed her face. Did she have dirt on her nose?

"What is it?" Odankot wondered.

"She's smiling," Jako-ki said.

It was true. Mary was smiling.

"If a husband can make Dehgewanus happy, then I must get one," Jako-ki said.

"Should I find one, too?" asked Odankot.

"If you smiled any more, you would outshine the sun," Jako-ki said.

The leaves fell into the Ohio and were carried south. The ducks and geese flew by overhead, too far away for even the strongest hunter's arrow. The men worked to make the canoes ready for the journey to the hunting ground at Scioto, where they spent the winter.

Then one morning, the oldest woman lit the council fire. "I had a dream," she said.

Everyone came to listen.

"I dreamed the snakes of the forest came together in a braid as thick as the council house and as long as a man can walk in a day. The braided snake slithered around our village. We couldn't hunt or fish. We couldn't go to tend our fields. The snake coiled itself tighter and tighter. Our land got smaller and smaller. Until it was a speck of dust."

"What does the dream mean?" Kau-jises-tau-ge-au said.

"It means we must fight to keep the Yengeese from squeezing our land," said the warrior chief.

"It means we need to return home," Hi-hi-ih said.

"But you are home," Sheninjee said.

"No. Our homeland is Ge-nun-de-wah. The great hill at Canandaigua Lake. Where our ancestors defeated the great serpent many, many years ago," Hi-hi-ih said.

"It's too far. It's beyond the place where the Ohio begins, beyond the Yengeese Fort Pitt. The journey will take more than a moon," Kau-jises-tau-ge-au declared.

"Some go every year to visit the rest of the tribe. I would like to see the great hill again. Then I would be closer to the Blue," the oldest woman said.

"Even if we go, how can we defeat the serpent?" asked a warrior.

"Soon the war between the Yengeese and the French will be over. The settlers will travel west on the soldiers' roads. They will burn our forests and take our fields," another warrior said.

"The Yengeese and the French snakes will join together to squeeze the Seneca."

"We must go home. If the tribe stands together, we can push back against the serpent. Besides"—Hi-hi-ih smiled—"my other daughters need to find husbands."

Both Jako-ki and Odankot agreed.

Mary already had a husband, however. She looked at Sheninjee. He didn't say anything. But by now she knew him well enough to read his thoughts. Ge-nun-de-wah might be an important place for the Seneca. But not for him.

The council fire burned for many days. Finally, the council agreed. Some would go northeast to Ge-nun-de-wah right now. The rest of the tribe would go south to the winter hunting ground at Scioto. They would go to Ge-nun-de-wah next spring.

The moon was dead when Jako-ki and Odankot loaded their canoe and prepared to paddle up the Ohio. Mary didn't want to say good-bye to them. The journey would be long. Many things could happen to them along the way—especially if the treaty was broken and Yengeese fought the Seneca again.

"What has happened to your smile?" Jako-ki teased.

"You will come to us soon," Odankot said.

"Of course. I have to approve of your husbands," Mary tried to joke.

"Maybe they'll give the gifts to Dehgewanus. What would you like? Oh, I know. A cradleboard," Jako-ki said.

"No!" Mary said.

"No?" Jako-ki said.

"I mean, not yet." Mary blushed.

"Ah. We'll miss you, Dehgewanus," said Jako-ki. "How else can we have strawberries all year?"

CHAPTER 22

GU SA' A GI
Winter—The Cold Has Arrived

hanges were coming. Only half the tribe went down the Ohio to the winter hunting grounds near Scioto. There were fewer people to feed. This was fortunate; the hunters had to travel farther to find deer. Kau-jises-tau-ge-au joked that they needed Ha-no-wa's squirrel for meat. But no one felt like laughing.

A runner brought news from the north. The Ottawa and other western tribes were angry. After the Yengeese had captured the French forts, the tribes had tried to live in peace. The Yengeese didn't show respect. They never gave gifts. They let their people burn the hunting grounds to make farms. They thought they were masters of the land because they had defeated the French. They had forgotten the land belonged to the tribes.

"Will there be war?" Kau-jises-tau-ge-au asked.

"How else can we make them stop?" the runner said.

"You can't," Sheninjee said.

Mary lay on her cot, listening to the voices of the men. Last year, there had been laughter. Now she heard them sharpening the stones on their axes. She placed her hand protectively over her belly. Yes, changes were coming.

Mary stayed awake until Sheninjee joined her. "Sheninjee? Will we go to Ge-nun-de-wah before the midwinter festival?"

He put his hand on her feet. "You have toes of ice here in this warm house. How will you travel all the way to the Seneca homeland in the winter?"

"I miss my sisters," Mary said.

"I do, too. I can hardly chew venison without Jako-ki's instructions. But what's the hurry?"

She wasn't sure how to tell him her news. "I need a cradleboard."

He placed his hand on her belly. "You are sure?"

"Yes. I have already felt the first kick."

"I'm so happy." Sheninjee touched Mary's cheek. "I didn't expect to be this happy. Of course we will go to your sisters—in the spring. Don't worry. I will make the cradleboard."

The Seneca used cradleboards to carry their children, as did many Native American tribes. The image above shows a baby from an unidentified tribe. *[LC-USZ62-121911]*

The next day, Sheninjee found a large log. He split it with a wedge. When he had a flat piece as long as his arm, he rubbed it with a rough stone to remove the sharp splinters. After the wood was as smooth as the ice on the pond, he bent a green branch into a half circle. He stuck the ends of the branch into holes at the top of the board. He made more holes down the sides for deerskin strips to tie the baby onto the board.

The tribe celebrated the midwinter festival. They cleared out the old ashes and chased evil away from the village.

After two more moons, Mary left the bark house and went to a small shack. Sheninjee couldn't go with her. Two women from the tribe helped Mary. Mary was frightened. Then she remembered that her own mother had given birth to her on a ship in the middle of the Atlantic Ocean.

The baby was a boy. The women wrapped him in soft skins and put him in Mary's arms. She whispered the names that still lived inside her heart.

"Thomas, Jane, Tom, John, Betsey, Mary, Matthew, Robert. Jemison."

Mary was sad to think that this boy would grow up without knowing he had another family, too. Then she smiled. She knew what she would do.

The next day, she brought the baby inside the bark house. The tribe was gathered around the fire.

"Here is your son," she told Sheninjee.

"Thank you for my son." He carefully took the tiny infant in his large hands. He put his cheek against the baby's thick, dark hair.

"He will be called Thomas Jemison," Mary said.

"Tom-as-jemi-sau?" Sheninjee had trouble speaking the unfamiliar sounds.

Mary let the baby grab her finger with his tiny hand. She was glad he was strong. He would need to be. "Thomas Jemison," Mary said.

For the rest of the winter, Mary kept Thomas Jemison close to her body. When spring came, she tied him to the cradleboard and went into the forest to collect the sweet sap from the trees. She propped the cradleboard against a tree while she boiled the sap over a hot fire. It took a long time to turn the clear liquid into golden maple syrup. When the baby got restless, she tied feathers to the branch that arched in front of his head.

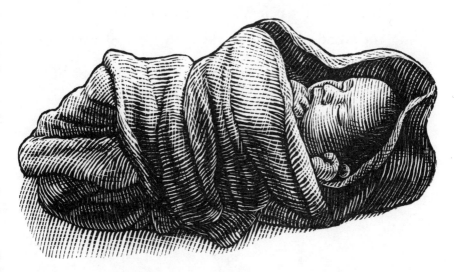

A black one for his aunt Jako-ki and a yellow one for Odankot. He smiled to see the feathers dance. But he would be much happier when his real aunts could fuss over him.

After the maple syrup had been collected, when the leaves on the trees were the size of a chipmunk's ears, the tribe left the winter camp and paddled up the Ohio.

Most of the canoes stopped at the village at Wiishto. Sheninjee had pelts to trade, so he, Mary, the baby, and Kau-jises-tau-ge-au continued on to a trading post. The men paddled. The canoe lurched forward with each stroke. Thomas Jemison pointed excitedly at a family of ducks tipping their heads under the water to find food.

"Ducks, Thomas Jemison." Mary loved rediscovering the wonders of the world with him. She felt as happy as if she was a baby, with no memories of the past and no worries about the future.

Then she noticed something else floating in the water. Bodies drifted toward the canoe. She couldn't see the men's faces, but they wore the clothes of white men.

"Guh, guh!" Thomas Jemison cried.

Mary tried to cover Thomas Jemison's eyes. He squirmed free. As the bodies floated closer, he started to whimper.

"Turn around," Sheninjee said. "We can't go to the trading post. We'll be blamed."

"But you didn't kill them," Mary said.

"Does that matter? The Yengeese will have their revenge," Sheninjee said.

"We need to trade the pelts." Kau-jises-tau-ge-au steered the canoe along the eastern edge of the river away from the bodies.

At the mouth of a creek was a log cabin. The men paddled hard to cross the river. Sheninjee jumped out and pulled the canoe up onto the sandy shore.

"Wait here while I see if the trader is there." Sheninjee took out his knife. Then he put it back in his belt. He held up his hands so that the trader could see he meant no harm.

Mary and Kau-jises-tau-ge-au waited. There was no sound except the river rushing past. Thomas Jemison pounded on the side of the canoe. Mary grabbed his hand.

"Shhh," she said.

The baby played with her fingers.

Sheninjee came out of the cabin. "No one is here."

Then they heard screaming from the woods. A white man tried to run away from three warriors who were hitting him with sticks. They laughed as the thorns tore into his skin.

"Shawnee. Like the ones who took you," Kau-jises-tau-ge-au said.

Mary looked at the warriors. She was glad she didn't recognize the ones who had killed her family.

"Help!" the white man cried in English.

The Shawnee pushed him to the ground and rubbed dirt in his wounds.

Sheninjee ran back to the canoe. He started to push it out into the water.

But Mary jumped out and ran toward the Shawnee. "Stop torturing that man! He can't hurt you. Let him go!" she screamed.

The Shawnee laughed. One raised his stick as if to strike Mary.

"Stop! I beg you!" Mary sobbed.

Sheninjee stood up and took out his knife.

The Shawnee looked at Sheninjee and then at

Kau-jises-tau-ge-au. The Shawnee threw his stick into the river. The others did the same. Their game was over. The white man ran off into the woods. The three Shawnee warriors went inside the trading post.

Sheninjee and Mary got into the canoe. Mary hugged Thomas Jemison to her heart and whispered, "Thomas, Jane, Tom, John, Betsey, Mary, Matthew, Robert."

The men paddled back to Wiishto. Kau-jises-tau-ge-au landed the canoe. Some of the tribe were still unloading their canoes and carrying bundles up to the village.

"What happened?" a woman asked.

"We must go to Ge-nun-de-wah tomorrow. There was trouble at the trading post. Now Yengeese warriors will come." Kau-jises-tau-ge-au hurried to the council house.

Sheninjee lifted his son up to the sky. Thomas Jemison laughed. He loved to fly in his father's hands. Then Sheninjee gave the baby to Mary. He smoothed her yellow hair behind her ear. "You go with your brother. I'll find you there after the winter hunting."

"But that is so many moons from now," Mary said.

"I need to trade my pelts. And get more. I have a family to look after now." Sheninjee stroked the short black hair on Thomas Jemison's head.

"Why can't we stay together?" asked Mary.

"Why can't the deer lie down to die at my feet?" Sheninjee said.

Mary thought of the sheep and cattle on Father's farm. "Some animals live inside fences. If you feed them, they grow until they're ready to be eaten."

"But I have no land that can be fenced," Sheninjee said.

Mary was silent.

Thomas Jemison grabbed the scarlet square of deerskin that hung from Sheninjee's neck. The baby studied it intently. Then he put it in his mouth.

Sheninjee took off the deerskin square and placed it over Mary's head. "I will come to you. I have much to teach Tom-as-jemi-sau."

"You need to teach me how to be brave, too," Mary said.

Sheninjee smiled. "Oh no, Dehgewanus. Life has already taught you that."

CHAPTER 23

GANA NA' GI

Summer—Red of Strawberries Has Come

After Mary Had Crossed Two Winters with the Seneca

Mary said good-bye to her husband and followed her brother toward the northeast, with her baby on her back. Her only comfort was that, at the journey's end, she would be reunited with Jako-ki and Odankot.

Kau-jises-tau-ge-au and Mary carried as much dried venison and corn as they could. After a week of walking, they had little food left. They discovered a native village. But they couldn't rest there. That tribe had fled after murdering some settlers who trespassed upon their land. Kau-jises-tau-ge-au found the places where that tribe had hidden beans, corn, and honey. They filled their pouches and continued on.

Thomas Jemison was one moon older. And bigger.

And heavier. Mary joked that before the journey ended, her son would carry her.

They came to Conowingo Creek. The waters were too high to wade across. Mary attempted to swim but the current forced her to turn back. She had to try three times before she reached the other side. From there to Che-ua-shung-gau-tau and after that to U-na-waum-gwa. They hoped to find more food, but early frosts had destroyed the corn. The tribes who lived there didn't have enough to feed themselves.

And so they walked on. Thomas Jemison was nine moons. Mary was tired of carrying him, tired of sleeping on the ground, tired of the cold rain that soaked her blankets. She worried they would never get to Ge-nun-de-wah. They would walk forever through the forest.

Finally, they came to the edge of a great lake.

"Canandaigua!" Kau-jises-tau-ge-au said.

Beyond the lake was a great hill that seemed to connect the earth to the Blue.

"Ge-nun-de-wah!" Kau-jises-tau-ge-au said.

They had finally reached the sacred place of the Seneca.

The lake was long; it took two more days to

journey around it to the Seneca village of Genishau. Many clans had built bark houses there. Mary saw the smoke from the fires and smelled the stew cooking. But all the faces she saw belonged to strangers. What if something had happened to her sisters on their journey? It had been so long since she had any news of them.

Mary sat down and waited while Kau-jises-tau-ge-au searched for their sisters and their mother. She took Thomas Jemison off her back, but she left him in his cradleboard. He looked around him with wide eyes, as if trying to figure out where he was and why his mother had brought him here. He began to wail.

"Don't cry." Mary was so exhausted. His sobs made her want to weep, too.

Just then, Jako-ki shouted, "Dehgewanus! What have you brought us? Where did that baby come from? Did you find him in the forest?"

Mary stood up to greet her sisters. She brushed the tears from her face.

"Poor Dehgewanus, look how tired you are. You've come such a long way. But we're very glad to have our sister with us again," Odankot said.

"Corn, bean, squash." Jako-ki pinched Thomas Jemison's cheek. "And is this the little rabbit who tries to eat our harvest?"

Odankot let the baby hold her finger. "He is a beautiful boy. What's his name?"

"Thomas Jemison," Mary said.

"Tom-as-jemi-sau?" Odankot tried to repeat.

"Dehgewanus will not say why she chose that name or what it means," Kau-jises-tau-ge-au said.

"Tom-as-jemi-sau doesn't sound Seneca," Jako-ki said.

"I'm sure the Great Spirit guided our sister," Odankot said.

Mary nodded. But she worried that name would make life difficult for her son.

"You have a handsome cradleboard," Jako-ki said. "I guess my husband will have to give you another gift."

"Do you have a husband?" asked Mary.

Jako-ki drew a line across her mouth with her finger.

"Not yet. She is still practicing to be silent," Odankot said.

———

After the midwinter festival, Jako-ki and Odankot both brought husbands into the bark house. Mary said Kau-jises-tau-ge-au should receive the gifts. All she wanted was her own husband to come soon.

Sheninjee didn't arrive in time for the Maple Sugar Festival. He missed the Planting the Corn, the Strawberry, and the Bean Festivals. Mary was certain he would arrive for the Green Corn Festival. That was when they had met. Thomas Jemison was walking and learning to say many words. Soon he would need his father to teach him what Mary couldn't.

Thomas Jemison sat on the ground by the cooking fire. Mary was scraping the young kernels into a bark bowl. When she finished with the ear, she gave it to Ha-no-wa.

"The deer chews it first. Ha-no-wa the turtle chews it next. And then Tom-as-jemi-sau!" Ha-no-wa gave the cob to Thomas Jemison. He stuck the end into his mouth.

Jis-ta-ah turned the cob sideways and gave it back. "This is how you eat it."

Thomas Jemison studied the cob and once again stuck the end into his mouth.

"He wants to do things his own way," Odankot said.

"He will be a great chief," Jako-ki declared.

"Or a great troublemaker," said Mary.

Everyone laughed.

Kau-jises-tau-ge-au came and stood by the fire. He didn't join the laughter.

"What's the matter? Why aren't you hunting for the Green Corn Festival? How can we feast on dried meat?" Jako-ki made a mound of corn, beans, meat, and apples and wrapped it in a corn husk. Mary tied the small bundle with a piece of grass. Odankot dropped the bundle into the kettle of boiling water.

"A runner has brought news from the west," Kau-jises-tau-ge-au said.

"We know. Chief Pontiac is leading the western tribes to fight the Yengeese at Fort Detroit," Jako-ki said.

"Jako-ki told her husband that if he goes, she will bake bread for another warrior," said Odankot.

"If I have to wear two braids again, Tom-as-jemi-sau will pull them." Jako-ki showed her neat loop of hair at the back of her neck.

"Dehgewanus," Kau-jises-tau-ge-au said softly. "That is not all the news. Sheninjee has gone to the Blue."

"No," Odankot gasped.

Mary didn't speak. She couldn't believe Sheninjee had died.

"Was it the war?" asked Jako-ki.

"No. He got sick after we left him. He went to the Blue last summer."

Mary buried her face in her hands.

"You have a home in our bark house. We will look after you. Kau-jises-tau-ge-au will hunt for you. You and Tom-as-jemi-sau will be fine," Jako-ki said.

Odankot sat beside Mary and squeezed her sister's hand.

No one spoke.

Thomas Jemison threw the cob into the fire. It was too wet to burn. But no one took it out. They let its smoke take a message up to the Blue.

Thomas, Jane, Tom, John, Betsey, Mary, Matthew, Robert . . . Sheninjee.

CHAPTER 24

SISGE'HA

The Moon When Plants Are Growing

After Mary Had Crossed Four Winters with the Seneca

Winter came early that year, and it seemed especially long to Mary, but finally spring came. Sweet sap flowed in the maple trees. Tiny green leaves poked out from the gray branches. White blossoms became strawberries. These changes seemed like miracles to Thomas Jemison.

Early in the moon of sisge'ha, Mary was working in the cornfield. Thomas Jemison was no longer in his cradleboard. Jis-ta-ah had to keep him out of mischief—just as Mary had watched the children not so long ago.

The corn was as tall as Thomas Jemison. The squash plants almost reached between each stalk. The beans were growing, too. But they didn't know what to cling to. Mary twisted each vine around a stalk. "Hold on to your sister. Or you'll drown in the mud."

Jis-ta-ah sat at the edge of the forest, digging a hole with Thomas Jemison.

"We're planting, too, Dehgewanus," Jis-ta-ah said.

"What kind of seeds?" Mary asked.

Thomas Jemison held up a white stone and a red stone.

"You never know what will grow." Mary smiled and turned to work in a new row.

At the edge of the field closest to the village stood a man named John Van Sice. He had a pointed reddish beard. He often came to the Seneca village to get meat or skins. He never used to pay any attention to Mary. She had nothing to trade. But he was watching her now.

Several moons ago, the Yengeese and the French had finally agreed to end their war. The French had lost. They had to give up all their territory in North America. The Yengeese claimed everything from the Atlantic Ocean to the Mississippi River. Unfortunately, neither the French nor the Yengeese had remembered to give the tribes a share of the land. Still, the Seneca were glad that there was peace.

Since the war was over, the Yengeese king wanted the tribes to return the people who had been kidnapped during the war. The king would pay to redeem any prisoner brought to a Yengeese fort.

John Van Sice had offered to help the Seneca chiefs get guns and kettles in exchange for their prisoners. Now he stared at Mary as he took a drink from a wineskin.

Mary nervously bent a vine around a stalk. The vine broke off. She looked at the plant in her hand. Without roots, it would die.

Van Sice took another drink from his wineskin. He closed the top. Then he walked purposefully toward her. Was he going to take her straight to Fort Niagara?

Mary panicked. She couldn't fight him. She was alone in the field. So she ran.

"Stop!" Van Sice shouted in English.

Mary grabbed her son and fled into the woods.

"Where are you going, Dehgewanus?" Jis-ta-ah shouted after her.

Mary had no breath to answer. Besides, she had no idea where she was going. She just wanted to get away from Van Sice.

She ran through brambles and up hills. She ran until each breath rasped inside her chest. Thomas

Jemison was crying. He didn't understand why his mother was acting this way. She couldn't explain.

She looked back toward the village. Had Van Sice followed her? She couldn't see or hear him. Was it safe to go back? What if he was behind those rocks, waiting to grab her?

Thomas Jemison was heavy. It was hard to carry him, but she had to keep going. She crossed a wide path. Then she saw a log cabin in the middle of a clearing. She stopped to listen. She didn't hear any human sounds. There was no smoke from a cooking fire, just a smell of old ashes. She came closer.

Part of a wall was burned. The door dangled from one hinge. The stone chimney had leaves at the top. A squirrel had made a nest. No one else lived in the cabin now.

She put Thomas Jemison down on a stump. "I'm going to look for food."

He grabbed hold of her tunic. "Mama?"

"Wait here. I'll be right back." She hoped she looked calmer than she felt.

She pushed through the door and entered the dark cabin. It took several moments for her eyes to adjust to the lack of light. A table had been tipped over. Broken dishes were scattered across the floor. She could almost see the warriors ransacking the Jemison house on that terrible day five years ago. She remembered the crack of the whip chasing her family from their home.

Thomas, Jane, Tom, John, Betsey, Mary, Matthew, Robert.

If Mary was redeemed, she could go back to the white world.

She picked up the pieces of a shattered dish and tried to fit them back together. She searched the floor for the missing piece.

"Mama?"

She looked up, startled. A little native boy stood in the doorway. He wore deerskin leggings. A fringe of black hair across his forehead almost hid his dark brown eyes. Two striped pheasant feathers stuck up from behind his ears.

He was her son.

She held out her hand. "Look, Thomas Jemison. This is a *plate*. This is a *table*." She had to use English words. The Seneca had no names for things they didn't have. "I know this place isn't very nice. But other cabins are. We could go someplace where you could have these things. Wouldn't you like that?"

He shook his head and refused to enter the cabin.

"Come here, Thomas Jemison."

She had given him a white name. But he wasn't white. She knew that even if some men had signed a treaty, there was still war in people's hearts. Most people weren't like Jako-ki and Odankot, who had chosen to forgive.

Mary put down the broken plate and clutched her pouch that held the scrap of lace. Would her mother want Mary to be redeemed to the white world?

Or would her mother want Mary to do what was best for her own child?

She looked around the cabin. She picked up a fork. Then she let it fall back to the floor. What good was a fork without food and a family to share that food with? Mary and Thomas Jemison had a family. They should stay with them.

She walked out of the shadows. She decided not to worry about Van Sice. Her Seneca family wouldn't let him redeem her. "Come, Thomas Jemison. Let's go home."

Thomas Jemison held her hand and led her back into the forest.

———✦———

When they got back to the village, Mary could see the smoke from the council fire. She wondered what the chiefs were discussing.

Jako-ki and Odankot were pounding corn outside the bark house. Mary gave Thomas Jemison a bowl of mush. He ate happily.

"I had to run away from Van Sice. I was afraid he would redeem me," Mary said.

"He took some other prisoners to Fort Niagara," Odankot said.

"Then he's gone." Mary sighed with relief. But her sisters still looked worried. "What's wrong?"

"The warrior chief wants to redeem you himself," Jako-ki said.

"What?" cried Mary. "Would he really do that?"

"Kau-jises-tau-ge-au is persuading the chiefs to let you stay," Odankot said.

They looked toward the council fire. Its smoke rose up to the sky in a black column. Then, even though the wind was barely blowing, the dark smoke drifted back toward the three sisters.

"What if they don't listen to Kau-jises-tau-ge-au?" Mary asked.

"Of course they will listen. Our brother speaks well," said Odankot.

"So do kettles and new rifles," Jako-ki said.

Then they heard Kau-jises-tau-ge-au shouting.

"Loud noises never win arguments. I told our brother to let me speak." Jako-ki pounded the corn angrily.

"But, Jako-ki, women cannot speak at the council fire. You know that," said Odankot.

The war chief shouted back.

"That is *not* a good sign," Jako-ki said.

"What should I do?" Mary picked up Thomas Jemison.

"I don't know, but I think you should hide while we figure out what to do," said Jako-ki.

"But we just got back." Mary didn't have the strength to run away again.

"Stay in the weeds until dark. If the warrior chief plans to redeem you, I will leave a corn cake at the door. If you find a cake, you must run all the way to the spring. Wait there for me," Jako-ki said.

Mary was too upset to move.

Thomas Jemison whimpered. Odankot patted the little boy's cheek.

But Jako-ki said, "Go!"

Mary didn't need to be told again. She ran to a patch of tall weeds that grew in a dry ditch. She lay down and pulled leaves over herself and Thomas Jemison. Then she waited. Darkness settled around her. After Thomas Jemison fell asleep, she left him in the ditch and silently crept back between the bark houses.

Mary could smell the stew that others had eaten for their meals. Bread was burning. Someone had

forgotten to take a corn cake out of the fire. Maybe
Jako-ki had learned she didn't need to leave the corn
cake. Maybe the warrior chief changed his mind.
Maybe she could stay. As she tiptoed through the
shadows, she heard voices from the other clans' houses.
Someone sang a baby to sleep. Someone snored.
Someone told the story of how the chipmunk got its
stripes.

All was silent inside Mary's bark house. The moon
hadn't risen yet. It was too dark to see. She knelt down
to pat the ground with her hands. She felt the dirt and
little rocks. She found a tall feather that must have
come loose from Kau-jises-tau-ge-au's hat. And then
her hand touched the soft corn cake.

She bit her lip. Tears came to her eyes. How could
the warrior chief want to redeem her? She stumbled
toward the ditch. Then she came back to put the cake
in her pouch. She would need the food if she had to
survive without her family.

Once more, she picked up Thomas Jemison. The
sleepy child didn't want to hang on to her back, so she
had to carry him in her arms. She walked quickly and
quietly as she returned to the forest. She had to be

more careful. This time she wasn't hiding from a white man. The ones looking for her would be Seneca.

The path to the spring was worn smooth by many feet. Mary pushed through the brush where she could stay hidden. When a branch scratched Thomas Jemison, he started to cry. She kissed his forehead and hoped that would comfort him. She couldn't stop until she got to the spring. She hoped she would be safe there. Would she ever be safe anywhere?

"Go home," Thomas Jemison whimpered.

"Shhh." She hushed him, but she felt like crying, too. She didn't want to be back in the woods. How many days had she been here? How many years? It felt like she had been wandering forever since the Shawnee warriors had kidnapped her.

Her foot slipped in the mud. She stood still. She heard the water bubbling up from the ground. At least she had found the spring.

She put Thomas Jemison down on a dry place. She knelt and dipped her hand under the water. She drank from her palm. She had no gourd. She had no pewter mug. She had nothing.

She had lost her family. She had lost her husband.

She thought she had made a new home with the Seneca, but she hadn't. The warrior chief wanted to redeem her—for kettles and guns.

Where could she go? How could she live? How could she take care of her son? She had no idea. She lay right where she was on the damp ground. She was so tired. She wanted to sleep forever. Maybe that would be the best thing for her to do.

Soon a gray light spread through the forest. The birds were chattering and singing. They welcomed the day.

Thomas Jemison whimpered. "Mama?"

Her son was hungry. She sat up. She took the corn cake out of her pouch. She tried to save half for later. But Thomas Jemison put it all in his mouth. His cheeks were as round as a chipmunk's. Mary watched him chew. Then she cupped her hand, dipped it in the spring, and let him drink water from her palm.

"No cup," she said.

He didn't care. He sat by the spring and played in the mud, laughing with delight. Then he offered her a handful of wet leaves. Mary took the leaves from him.

He put his hand to his mouth, as if she should eat the leaves.

"You're right, Thomas Jemison. We can find food here." Mary pretended to eat the leaves.

The woods would provide for her just as they did for the Seneca. She had learned a lot from them. But had she learned enough?

Suddenly, Mary heard the crack of broken twigs. Someone was coming. Someone white—who didn't know how to walk silently in the woods. Or someone who had no need to be silent because he had nothing to fear.

Mary had expected Jako-ki to come with a plan. But it was Kau-jises-tau-ge-au.

"Dehgewanus, you must return to the village. The warrior chief is taking the prisoners to Fort Niagara to be redeemed."

"Oh no!" Mary cried. Thomas Jemison clutched at her tunic.

Kau-jises-tau-ge-au stared at her. Then he said softly, "Aren't you glad to return to your people?"

"Seneca are my people," Mary said.

"You would choose to stay?" asked Kau-jises-tau-ge-au.

"Yes," Mary answered.

Kau-jises-tau-ge-au sighed. "Then I'm sorry. But the warrior chief needs guns."

"Isn't the war over?" asked Mary.

"The white man's war is over, but we must be prepared to fight. We still don't own our land."

Kau-jises-tau-ge-au picked up Thomas Jemison and carried the little boy on his shoulders. They walked back toward the village on the path. There was no need to hide anymore.

Mary held her head high as her brother led her toward the council house. It was getting late in the day. Maybe the warrior chief wouldn't want to take the prisoners to Fort Niagara until tomorrow morning. Then Mary could have one last night in the bark house with her sisters.

"Dehgewanus!" Jako-ki called to her from outside their bark house.

"Where are you going?" cried Odankot.

"To the council house," Kau-jises-tau-ge-au said. "The warrior chief wants her."

"He isn't there. He has taken the prisoners to Fort Niagara," Jako-ki said.

"He didn't wait to take Dehgewanus?" exclaimed Kau-jises-tau-ge-au.

"Jako-ki told him Dehgewanus couldn't be redeemed. She isn't a prisoner. She's our sister," Odankot said.

"Women can't speak at the council fire. They can only sit and listen." Kau-jises-tau-ge-au was taken aback.

"My sharp tongue should be good for something," said Jako-ki.

"Did the warrior chief listen?" Mary asked.

"Our mother, Hi-hi-ih, said if he didn't, she would knock off his horns and make someone else chief," Jako-ki said.

"Then I can stay!" Mary hugged Jako-ki.

"The bean is strangling the corn." Jako-ki laughed.

"Corn bean squash!" Thomas Jemison shouted.

"He is hungry," said Mary.

"How can he be? I left you such a nice corn cake!" Jako-ki said.

They all laughed.

Thomas Jemison grabbed his aunts' hands and led them into the bark house.

"Maybe we can fight for our land without guns," Mary said.

"Maybe the Yengeese will make a new treaty," said Kau-jises-tau-ge-au.

"And keep their promises," Mary added.

"When that day comes, Dehgewanus, you should have your own land because you have chosen to stay with the Seneca," Kau-jises-tau-ge-au said.

"When that day comes." Mary hoped it would be soon. But she wondered how many wars would be fought before that could happen.

EPILOGUE

Two girls and a boy stood on the lowest rail of the fence. Alice and Eliza were careful to keep their white pinafores away from the rough wood. George's trousers were already splattered with mud.

"How do you know the White Woman of Genesee lives there?" asked George.

"Mother says a man wrote a book about her," Alice said.

"Why is she called the White Woman? Isn't she a red Indian?" Eliza asked.

They looked at the house. It was about twenty feet long. The walls were made of square timber. The roof

The cabin that belonged to Mary Jemison's daughter, Nancy Jemison. It was built on the Gardeau Flats, the land granted to Mary at the Treaty of Big Tree. *[Tom Cook and Tom Breslin, Letchworthparkhistory.com]*

was shingled. Smoke came up from a stone chimney and faded into the blue sky. Beyond the house was a barn. A herd of cattle grazed in the meadow.

"She can't be a red Indian. She has too many cattle," George said.

"And why can't an Indian have cattle?"

An old woman in moccasins had snuck up silently behind them. Her white hair was tied with a strip of deerskin. Her dress was brown cloth. A small pouch hung from a strip of deerskin around her neck.

The children jumped down from the fence so quickly that Eliza skinned her elbow on the rail.

"You better let me tend your scrapes. Come inside.

I know you're curious." Mary smiled and led them past a big garden. Corn, beans, and squash plants were just beginning to grow.

The children followed Mary into the house. There was hardly any furniture. A bench was against one wall. Several cots were in the corner. Baskets and red ears of dried corn hung from the rafters.

Mary pointed to the bench. The children sat in a row. Mary dipped a soft cloth in a bucket of water and handed it to Alice. After Alice had cleaned Eliza's wound, Mary offered her a little wooden bowl. "This paste will ease the sting."

"What is it?" Alice peered at it suspiciously.

"Lavender mixed with beeswax," Mary said.

"It smells nice." Eliza rubbed some on her elbow. "That's much better."

Mary put away the bowl and sat on the floor.

"Are you Indian or white?" George asked.

Mary smiled. "That is a good question. I was born white. But when I was fifteen, I was taken from my home by Shawnee warriors. I was adopted by two Seneca sisters. I married a Lenape named Sheninjee. After he died of sickness, I married the Seneca chief Hiokatoo. I have eight children, thirty-nine grandchildren, and fourteen great-grandchildren who were all raised Seneca. So I ask you. Am I white?"

"No," said George.

"Yes," Alice said.

"Maybe," said Eliza.

Mary looked at her hands. Her fingers were twisted like the roots of a tree. "Mostly I know I'm old."

A portrayal of an elderly Mary Jemison from a 1905–1906 postcard. [Tom Cook and Tom Breslin, Letchworthparkhistory.com]

"Is this your house?" asked George.

"Yes. And my land. In fact, if you're the son of William Jones, then your father is my tenant," Mary said.

"He is?" George was surprised.

"How could an Indian get land?" Alice wondered.

Mary sighed. "It wasn't easy. After the Revolutionary War, the new states drew their borders right through our hunting grounds and across our fields. The western tribes wanted to fight for their share of the land. The Seneca tribe decided to make a treaty with the new country."

"The United States of America," George said.

"The Seneca chiefs and women went to Big Tree to light the council fire. I went, too. My brother, Kaujises-tau-ge-au, had said I should get my own land, after I chose to stay with the Seneca."

"You *chose* to stay with the Seneca?" asked Eliza.

"Yes. They are my family." Mary showed the children her moccasins. One had a beaded blackbird. The other had a sun. "My sisters walk with me every step I take."

"Is Big Tree where you got the land?" George asked.

"The council fire was lit. There were many speeches. There are *always* many speeches. The Seneca are very good at talking. A man named Thomas Morris gave pieces of land to all the chiefs. Then I was brought before him. I remembered how the Lenape had been cheated. I knew my husband Sheninjee would not want that to happen to me."

Mary placed her hand on the faded red square of deerskin.

"I asked Thomas Morris if I could have my corn patch. 'Where is your corn patch?' he asked. I said, 'Oh, it's just that little piece of land between the creek and the ridge and the river.' 'That can't be much,' he said. So he let me have it. When it was

The Genesee River as it runs through Letchworth State Park, photographed sometime between 1895 and 1910. *[LC-DIG-det-4a16418]*

surveyed, they found it was eighteen thousand acres." Mary laughed.

"You cheated," George said.

Mary shook her head. "Thomas Morris thought I was an old squaw in a dirty blanket. He thought he could cheat *me*—but I was tired of walking through the forest. I wanted to have a home."

She stood up and poked the fire until bright flames leapt up from the gray ashes.

Laughter came from outdoors. A boy and a girl brought baskets of strawberries into the house. Their clothes were made of cloth, but they had feathers in their hair.

"Ak-so! Shes-a-ha!" the boy said.

"At-e-o," Mary said. "These are my great-grandchildren, Jane and John. Neh-teh-neh. Share the strawberries with our guests."

Jane offered the basket. George, Eliza, and Alice each took a handful of berries.

George started to eat.

"Nee-yah-wenh," John said.

"Yes, we must give thanks." Mary sprinkled some dried leaves on the fire. She waved the smoke up the chimney and all the way to the Blue.

The children prayed. They frowned when they heard the others use unfamiliar words.

But Mary knew they were all grateful in their own ways. She said her own thanks. "Nee-yah-wenh, Great Spirit. Thank you, Ha-wen-ni-yu."

Every moment of every day, Mary was grateful for her journey from that ship on a storm-tossed sea, through hundreds of miles of woods, and finally to this home. She was especially grateful to *all* her loved ones—mothers, father, sisters, brothers, husbands, sons, daughters, grandchildren, and great-grandchildren who had helped her.

It was true what the Seneca said: Corn, bean, squash. Dio-heh-ko. They sustain us!

AUTHOR'S NOTE

One thing only marred my happiness, while I lived with them [the Seneca] on the Ohio; and that was the recollection that I had once had tender parents, and a home that I loved. . . . If I had been taken in infancy, I should have been contented in my situation. Notwithstanding all that has been said against the Indians . . . it is a fact that they are naturally kind, tender and peaceable towards their friends, and strictly honest; and that those cruelties have been practised, only upon their enemies, according to their idea of justice.

—A NARRATIVE OF THE LIFE OF MRS. MARY JEMISON
BY JAMES E. SEAVER

Mary Jemison was a real person. She got the chance to tell her own story when she was interviewed by James E. Seaver in 1823. His book, *A Narrative of the Life of Mrs. Mary Jemison*, is still in print. Mary remembered an amazing amount—considering that, after she began living with the Seneca, she had no way to write down anything or even know what year it was. Perhaps as a result, some of her dates didn't agree with historical facts. I made adjustments to her calendar in those cases. But every main event that I describe was taken from Seaver's book.

A person's life is more than just what happens. In Mr. Seaver's book, Mary says she grew to love her Seneca sisters and her husband Sheninjee. She also describes her depression after losing her family. I never contradicted what I knew about Mary, but I did use my imagination when I wrote about many of her other feelings.

Mary never names her Seneca sisters or describes their personalities, but I couldn't tell Mary's story without bringing those sisters to life. Their love for Mary is one of the most important parts of Mary's history. I also invented names for Mary's Seneca mother and the children Mary befriends. Mary's husbands and brother are identified in Seaver's book. And she really did name her Seneca children after the Jemisons.

Like many tribes, the Seneca have an oral tradition. Their rich history and culture are best known to them. Mary describes much about the Seneca way of life in Seaver's book. I was also able to learn more about them by reading *The Seneca World of Ga-no-say-yeh (Peter Crouse, White Captive)* by Joseph A. Francello; *Iroquois Music and Dance: Ceremonial Arts of Two Seneca Longhouses* by Gertrude P. Kurath; "The Seasons of the Senecas" by Linda Pascatore; and *Seneca Indian Myths* by Jeremiah Curtin. The Seneca creation myth that I retell comes from

Curtin's book. The Seneca words I use also come from Curtin's book, as well as from *Seneca Morphology and Dictionary* by Wallace L. Chafe.

There may be errors in my attempt to describe the Seneca way of life, but I hope that I've conveyed my admiration for their compassion, their oratory, their stories, their wise leaders, and their sense of humor.

A statue of Mary Jemison erected in Letchworth State Park. *[Photographer Ryan Hargett, licensed under a Creative Commons Attribution—ShareAlike 3.0 Unported License]*

Seaver's book doesn't say why the war chief chose not to redeem Mary. I decided to allow Jako-ki, who I imagined as being outspoken, to defend Mary's wish to remain with the tribe. Since the sisters loved Mary, I know they would have done whatever they could to keep her with them. But Seneca women didn't usually speak at council fires. The elder women had the power to select the chiefs and to take away the chiefs' authority—or, as the Seneca say, "Knock the horns off."

Mary wasn't the only prisoner taken during the French and Indian War. Many people were killed or captured from 1754 until 1763. The name for the war is misleading. At that time, England fought France in various locations all around the world. Many tribes, including the Seneca, initially sided with the French. The tribes hoped to prevent more colonists from settling on their land. But as the British began overpowering the French, the tribes thought it wisest to switch sides. In the end, it didn't matter. When England and France signed their treaty to end the war, they completely disregarded the tribes who had been there first.

Mary Jemison did receive 18,000 acres at the Treaty of Big Tree in 1797. But Mary was luckier than many members of the tribe. The main purpose of that treaty was to sell most of the land the Seneca claimed, except for twelve tracts of land that became reservations. The Seneca tribe still lives there.

Like many Native Americans, the Seneca have faithkeepers. They maintain the tribe's values and traditions to share its wisdom as well as the gifts of the earth. The faithkeeper at the Cattaraugus Reservation is G. Peter Jemison, an eighth-generation descendant of Mary Jemison.

GLOSSARY

OF TERMS

ak-so: A Seneca word for "grandmother."

aller (verb): A French word meaning "to go."

arrêter (verb): A French word meaning "to stop."

at-e-o: A Seneca word meaning "be friends."

Blue: How the Seneca refer to heaven.

bouffe (noun): A French word meaning "food."

crossed the winter: How the Seneca refer to the passing of a year.

Dehgewanus: A Seneca name meaning "two falling voices."

dio-heh-ko: The Seneca word for "corn, bean, and squash"; the word actually means "they sustain us."

dion-dot: A Seneca word meaning "tree."

Fort Duquesne: A French fort built in 1754 at the point where the Allegheny and the Monongahela Rivers form the Ohio River. Pittsburgh, Pennsylvania, is now located there.

Fort Necessity: A small fort in western Pennsylvania built by Colonel George Washington in 1754. After the French attacked, Washington surrendered the fort on July 4, 1754.

Fort Pitt: A fort built by the British in 1759 on the site of Fort Duquesne.

Ge-nun-de-wah: A Seneca name meaning "Great Hill"; a large mountain at Canandaigua Lake in the western part of New York State; the origin of the Seneca tribe.

Ha-no-wa: A Seneca name meaning "turtle."

Ha-wen-ni-yu: The Seneca name meaning "Great Spirit."

he-eh: A Seneca word meaning "no."

Hi-hi-ih: A Seneca name meaning "owl."

homme (noun): A French word for "man."

Jako-ki: A Seneca name meaning "blackbird."

Jis-ta-ah: A Seneca name meaning "grasshopper."

ka-jih: A Seneca word meaning "come."

kah-kaw: A Seneca word meaning "moon."

Kau-jises-tau-ge-au: A Seneca name meaning "black coals."

look: How the Seneca describe a distance that is as far as one can look.

Monongahela: A river 128 miles long that flows north from West Virginia to join the Allegheny River and form the Ohio River at Pittsburgh, Pennsylvania.

moon: How the Seneca refer to a month.

nee-yah-wenh: A Seneca word meaning "thank you."

neh-teh-neh: A Seneca word meaning "give food to."

Odankot: A Seneca name meaning "sunshine."

On les prend?: A French phrase meaning "Shall we take them?"

On les tue?: A French phrase meaning "Shall we kill them?"

prendre (verb): A French word meaning "to take."

sachem: A North American tribal chief, especially of a confederation of tribes.

shes-a-ha: A Seneca word meaning "wild strawberry."

Six Nations: A confederation of the Seneca, Oneida, Onondaga, Mohawk, Cayuga, and Tuscarora tribes. It was formed as the Iroquois Confederacy in the sixteenth century to encourage peace and lawful agreements among the tribes. Benjamin Franklin and other Founding Fathers were inspired by the Six Nations when they helped establish the United States of America.

teh-ya-kwa-teh-neh-tey: A Seneca phrase meaning "we are sisters."

ti-ti: A Seneca word meaning "blue jay."

toh-kes: A Seneca word meaning "yes."

Treaty of Big Tree: An agreement signed on September 15, 1797, between the Seneca tribe and the United States government at Big Tree, near Geneseo, New York. The Seneca sold 1.3 million acres of land to the United States for $100,000. Some Seneca chiefs were paid signing bonuses and given allowances. Mary Jemison was given land in western New York. But the rest of the Seneca had to live on the Tonawanda, Allegany, Cattaraugus, Tuscarora, and Buffalo Creek Reservations.

Treaty of Easton: An agreement signed in October 1758 between the British and the chiefs of the Oneida, Onondaga, Mohawk, Cayuga, Tuscarora, Seneca, Shawnee, and Lenape tribes. The tribes agreed to be allies of the British for the rest of the French and Indian War. In return, Pennsylvania and New Jersey recognized the tribes' hunting grounds in the Ohio River valley. The British also promised not to allow any more settlements west of the Appalachian Mountains.

tuer (verb): A French word meaning "to kill."

vouloir (verb): A French word meaning "to want."

Walking Purchase: An agreement made in 1737 between the colony of Pennsylvania and the Lenape tribe. The Lenape had agreed to sell a section of land with a boundary of as much as a man could walk in a day and a half. But the colonists used fast runners on a cleared path and so forced the Lenape to vacate an area that was 1,200,000 acres of land, nearly twice as much as the Lenape expected to lose.

wampum: A belt made of dark- and light-colored shells arranged in a specific pattern. The belt can be used as part of a treaty or as a historical record.

Yengeese: The tribes' word for "English colonists."